P9-EDS-988

A CABIN FOR THE MARY CHRISTMAS

by the same author

SUDDEN VOYAGE

A CABIN FOR THE

Amrein, Vera R.
A cabin for the Mary
Christmas /
c1955.
33305217088628
HQ   02/05/09

Mrs. **VERA R. AMREIN**

ILLUSTRATED BY PETER SPIER

MARY CHRISTMAS

HARC   V YORK

This book is from the:

santa clara
county
library district

© COPYRIGHT, 1955, BY VERA R. AMREIN

All rights reserved, including the right to reproduce this book or portions thereof in any form.

first edition

LIBRARY OF CONGRESS CATALOG CARD NUMBER: 55-8668

PRINTED IN THE UNITED STATES OF AMERICA

Santa Clara County Free Library
San Jose, Calif.

FOR POLLY

306682

A CABIN FOR THE MARY CHRISTMAS

CHAPTER 1

Nora and Toby Brice were shivering on the dank, gloomy train platform, their eyes strained toward the gates at the head of the long stairway that were due to clang shut at any moment. Toby had hunched his shoulders and turned up the collar of his pea jacket, but now his blond, cropped head emerged like a turtle's as he looked up at the burly conductor standing alongside them.

"How much more time have we?" he asked him.

The conductor, who apparently had been deeply absorbed in his own thoughts, came to life with a slight start and hooked his watch out of his vest pocket. "Just enough fer ye t' be skedaddlin' inside if yer goin' along with me," he said, squinting at it.

"Couldn't you hold up the train for just another minute?" Nora pleaded. "We're expecting our brother."

The conductor slowly shook his head, then pointed. "Could that be him now?" He had caught sight of a long-legged boy, squeezing through the closing gates.

"That's him!" Toby shouted. "Mark! Hustle it up, goof!"

Mark plunged down the stairs hugging a bulky oblong parcel to his chest with one arm and bumping a suitcase and a duffel bag behind him.

The conductor waved toward the train, then cupped his hand and shouted, "Bo-oard!"

Mark got the idea and ducked into the nearest coach just seconds before the train jolted to a start.

"Now that's what ye call a pierhead leap in reverse!" The big conductor swung himself aboard the moving train and followed Nora and Toby. "You'd best be cuttin' along to him."

"We planned to meet in the coach ahead of the baggage car," Nora explained.

"Because our dog's tied up in there." Toby was tugging at one of the seats so that two would be facing. "Dink gets insulted if you try to put him in a carrier."

The conductor snapped his fingers. "Sure now an' ye're the ones who'll be stoppin' at the Fo'c's'le along with Mrs. Snow. She told me you was likely t' be on this train."

"That's us," said Toby.

"Me mind's takin' a holiday. I should have guessed who you was instanter, when I saw ye bring yer wee black Scottie aboard." The conductor took off his cap and ran his fingers through a mop of rust-colored hair plentifully sprinkled with white. "I was rememberin' I'm havin' a birthday this year same as always, an' so, after almost fifty years on the cars in one capacity or another, any day now the Long Island Railroad will be puttin' me out t' grass— an' me just reachin' me prime!" He sighed lugubriously, then drawing himself to his full height, went on, "Would you say, lookin' at big Conor O'Brien, that he was gettin' too old an' doddery t' handle a ticket punch?"

Nora and Toby carefully looked him up and down. Then Toby laughed.

"I'd hate to be behind any kind of a punch of yours," he said.

"Do you live in Kewanaka Bay, Mr. O'Brien?" A tiny

dimple showed in the corner of her mouth as Nora looked up at him.

"That I do. The finest little town on Long Island Sound."

"And the saltiest," Toby added. "Have you a boat?"

"Would I be choosin' Kewanaka t' live in if I had not? The *Monica* is the sweetest little fishin' boat that ever come out of Corbey's shipyard."

"We know Mr. Corbey, and Sam too," Nora said.

Conor O'Brien nodded. "Many's the bluefish young Sam and I have trolled fer together. T' think he's old enough t' be goin' t' college now— Maybe I am gettin' on."

"Sam said I caught the biggest blue he ever saw, last summer," said Toby.

"Did he now? Then it must have been a whopper."

"If you're a friend of Mrs. Snow's, how come we didn't meet you when we were in Kewanaka last summer?" Toby asked. "Gosh, we met practically everyone—of any importance, I mean."

"Maybe because when the fish are runnin', I spend my days off where they're runnin' thickest."

"Well, gosh," said Toby. "I should think you'd be glad they're retiring you. Then you can go fishing every day if you like."

Conor O'Brien scratched his head reflectively before jamming on his cap. "Maybe ye've got somethin' there, laddie." His blue eyes twinkled. "Well, I'd best be gettin' along t' give yer brother a hand with his luggage." He started up the aisle, then turned and cocked a bushy red eyebrow in Toby's direction. "Ordinarily I don't hold with breakin' the rules, but it's turrible cold in that baggage car, an' yer dog such a little feller." Balancing himself

6

with the grace of a dancer in the swaying train, the big man started up the aisle again.

Toby heaved himself to his feet, a grin spreading over his face. "Back in a sec," he flung over his shoulder to Nora.

But Nora grabbed hold of his pea jacket. "You'd better keep Dinghy hidden, just the same," she warned.

"I catch. Will do." Toby lurched his way to the baggage car and when he got back his arms were folded over his stomach which seemed to have filled out since he had left.

"Hi, Tubby!" Mark was there, still carefully clutching his paper-covered parcel and trying to shuck himself out of his topcoat with Nora's help. "Hi, Dink, old boy," he whispered, and the bulge under Toby's pea jacket wriggled a little.

Toby slid into the seat opposite the others, and easing out of his jacket, made a nest of it for the little black dog. "The conductor said we could keep him in here," he explained to Mark.

"I know. He told me."

"Did he tell you he lives in Kewanaka and knows Mrs. Snow?" Toby said.

"He did that, and what a sad thing it is t' be growin' old."

Mark sounded so much like the burly conductor, the others had to laugh.

"Whatever made you so late, Mark?" Nora was hanging up her polo coat, because now that the doors were shut, the coach was comfortably warm.

"I had to lock up the shop and return the key to Miss Munson. She and I were the only ones left in the school,

I guess, and she'd locked the office and gone off some place. I was just trying to shove the key under the door when she got back. Whew! I sure cut it fine. Did you get my ticket?"

"I have them." While Toby fumbled at his jacket to find the right pocket, he murmured to Dinghy to keep him quiet, though there was little need for caution. Except for them, the only passengers in their coach were two men who appeared to be dozing, and a woman with numerous packages piled alongside her which she was constantly counting and rearranging, and so, much too busy to pay them any attention.

The train was leaving the tunnel when the big conductor came back to them, carrying the rest of Mark's luggage which he stowed in the rack over their heads. "All hunky-dory?" he asked Toby as he took the tickets from him and winked, in a conspiratorial way, at the bundle beside him.

Toby winked back. "Do you know Ted Chase?" he asked, and when the big man had nodded, Toby smirked and fluttered his eyelashes. "Don't tell them I told you," he whispered hoarsely, "but Ted and Nora are—you know —*that way* about each other."

"Toby!" Nora glared at him.

"Do you know a skinny little thing with knobby knees and braces on her teeth?" Mark leaned back and put his feet up on the seat beside Toby. "I think her name is Floosie—no it's Flossie—Flossie Henderson."

Mr. O'Brien chuckled. "I've known Flossie since she was sailin' around in a pram instead of in that dinghy of hers."

8

Mark held up his middle and forefinger and snapped them together. "Well, Toby and Flossie are just like that."

"Why—why—" Toby spluttered, "why—why—"

"Now, now!" Conor O'Brien cut in soothingly, "no need gettin' pink around the gills. Young love is a beautiful thing."

Even Toby had to laugh at that.

"The high school's playin' a basketball game in Winbourne t'day." Conor O'Brien perched himself on the arm of the seat across the aisle from them. "The game should be over by the time we get there, so some of yer friends may be comin' aboard. Though the team an' the cheer leaders an' such go back in the school bus."

"Ted plays—" Nora began, then shot a glance at Toby, but he was saying:

"We didn't get a chance to let anyone but Mrs. Snow know that we were coming so soon, because we didn't know ourselves till yesterday. Did she tell you that we're going to be in Kewanaka until after New Year's?"

"She said somethin' about it, an' I've been wonderin' what kind of schools it could be that y' go to. Why, we're barely into December, an' our schools won't be closin' till just before Christmas."

"We wouldn't ordinarily be getting such a long vacation," Mark explained. "We all go to the same school, and some of the kids obliged by picking up a virus and spreading it around. When the teachers began coming down with it, they decided to close early."

"It's a sort of epidemic all over the city," Nora added. "So Father thought Kewanaka would be healthier for us right now. We were going to spend Christmas at the Fo'c's'le anyway."

"We'll have to make up the time though." Toby made a face. "We've had to bring all our books. My duffel bag weighs a ton. Nora and I left our stuff in the baggage car. Is that all right?"

"Sure, an' it will be fine there." Mr. O'Brien was eyeing the parcel that Mark was carefully balancing on his lap. "Let me put that up in the rack fer ye," he suggested. "It will be quite safe, an' it's a longish ride ye have."

But Mark shook his head. "I'd rather hang on to it. It's fragile."

The big man grunted. "Yer *lares* an' *penates* I have no doubt."

"No, it's a model of our sloop, *Scud*." Toby corrected him. "Mark made it in the shop at school. It's Father's Christmas present."

Mark and Nora burst out laughing.

"What did I say that was so funny?" demanded Toby.

"Perhaps it's me they're laughin' at." Mr. O'Brien was laughing too. "Speakin' the Latin tongue with me Irish brogue. *Lares* an' *penates* is household gods. Sam teaches me bits of Latin now an' then."

"I know a bit of Latin too." Toby folded back the pea jacket so that one of Dinghy's black ears and one beady eye could be seen. "*Cave canem!*" he said. "That means beware the dog."

Conor O'Brien reached into the bundle, and pulling out the little dog, held him up in front of him, then threw back his head in a Jovian roar as a pink tongue reached out to lick his face. "*Cave canem!*" he finally gasped. "Is that right? What a fierce little creature it is."

As Toby took him from Mr. O'Brien, he looked along the aisle for fear somebody might be watching. But the two men were still napping, and the woman was still counting her packages.

"Well, I'd best be about me business," Mr. O'Brien said after Dinghy was hidden away again. "After all, they haven't retired me yet."

Mark waggled his fingers after him, then turned his head and looked out the window. Long Island was having one of its least attractive December days. The streets in the town they were passing through glistened with dirty sludge, and in the dreary backyards, limp, grayish washes were flapping wetly from lines strung up over the lumpy half-frozen mud.

"It doesn't seem at all like the beginning of Christmas vacation," Toby grumbled. "Gosh, and I brought my skis along."

"Skis!" exclaimed Mark. "There are no mountains on Long Island."

"I thought if we had snow I could get in a little practice on Johnny Cake Hill in case Father can take us to that ski place in New Hampshire over Washington's birthday."

"By the way," Nora said. "I had a letter from Wisconsin this morning—from Edith Weaver. She says they've already had lots of skiing and skating out there."

"I thought I was going to miss the old school." Mark turned his eyes away from the uninviting landscape. "But I really like living in the city as long as we can get away sometimes like this and can sail on the Sound all summer."

Nora nodded. "I like New York too, there's so much to see and do. But even if I didn't, I'd be willing to put up with it just to be living with Father again. And for other reasons I like day school better than boarding school."

"Oh, my gosh, will you look at that!" Toby was again gazing out the window, and now rain was streaming down the panes in slanting gray lines.

"It might turn to snow," Nora said.

"Fat chance!" Toby fumbled at the pea jacket again and came up with a candy bar which he held out. "Want one? I've got more."

Nora and Mark shook their heads so Toby peeled it, and without taking his eyes off the window, began to munch. He watched the gray panes so long that before he was half-way through his second candy bar, the grayness grew deeper and deeper, and then he was asleep.

It was really dark outside when he woke up. Nora was shaking him.

"We'll be coming into Winbourne any minute now," she said. "I thought you'd like to be out on the platform in case anyone we know is there."

Toby sat up with sudden energy and shook his head to clear it, then realized that he had been lying on the seat with his jacket for a pillow. "Where's Dink?" he asked.

"Mark has him outside. Every time the train jolted, we thought you'd break your neck so we stretched you out. He decided the model would be safe enough up there." She nodded toward the rack. "He wedged it between the duffel bag and the suitcase."

"Yow!" Toby gave a great yawn. "Did I miss anything?"

"Nothing exactly world-shattering. People got off and people got on. Sometimes it rained and sometimes it didn't. Even the glimpses of the Sound were dreary. Between the mist and the rain, you couldn't tell where the sea left off and the sky began. We did talk a little with

Mr. O'Brien about fishing, and I think Dinghy's rather enjoyed the trip. Mark took him for a run at some of the comparatively dry stops and— What are you looking for?"

Toby was feeling around on the seat and peering at the floor. "My cocoanut bar. I don't think I finished it."

"I finished it for you." Nora was putting on her coat. "And I have the others in my pocket. Between you and Dink, they'd have made an awful mess. Climb into your jacket and come on."

The train was beginning to slow down when they joined Mark and Dinghy on the platform. Mr. O'Brien was standing on the lowest step in his long black slicker that was shining with rain. He was ready to swing to the ground when the train should come to a halt.

"Will ye look at that now!" he exclaimed, leaning far out. "There's quite a crowd ridin' back with us t'day."

Then the others could see a sea of umbrellas and people, milling under the dim station lights.

"Hi, kids!" a voice rang out from the crowd.

"It's Ted!" Mark and Nora exclaimed together.

"There's Spike Adams!" shrilled Toby. "Hi-yah, Spike!"

"And Charley Adams too," Mark said. "Who won the game, Charley?"

"Charles Spenser Adams, of course—practically single-handed."

Mark and Toby booed as the laughing crowd scattered to climb aboard, and Dinghy added his yelps to the din.

"I caught a glimpse of Pen Strong." Nora was laughing too, as Mark herded them into the coach so as to make room for the passengers who were swarming up the steps. "It looks as though Mrs. Snow might have spread the word around that we were taking this train."

CHAPTER 2

F OR A WHILE the coach ahead of the baggage car had the earmarks of all happy reunions, as Mark, Nora and Toby bombarded their summer friends with questions and answered theirs, with everybody talking at once.

However, it had become fairly quiet again by the time the big conductor had finished punching his tickets. "Now that yer givin' yer throttles a rest," he said, "I'll sit me down an' rest fer a bit."

"Sit here next to Pen, Mr. O'Brien." A boy with a nice grin got up from the seat across the aisle from the Brices.

"Thank you, Ted. Hello, Penelope. I'm not so old I don't fancy sittin' next to a pretty girl."

"Blarney, Mr. O'Brien—pure blarney. I look like a drowned rat, and you know it." Pen Strong was trying to fluff up her wet hair with her fingers.

"Squat here, Ted." Mark patted the arm rest next to him.

"I'm sorry!" A girl, who had been walking down the aisle, tripped over Ted's feet and would have landed in Toby's lap if Mark had not caught hold of her.

"Take my seat." Mark got out of the way, and the girl dropped into it.

"Thanks. My sea legs are a bit rusty, I guess."

"I humbly apologize for my outsized hoofs." Ted Chase

stood up and leaned on the back of the seat. "This is Star Thurston, kids. Her father's the new principal of the high school."

"Weeps! You must have to watch your step when she's around," remarked Toby.

"That's Nora Brice sitting alongside you," Ted went on. "And the gallant character who gave you his seat is her big brother, Mark. Pint-size over there is John Brice, Junior—but they call him Toby because—"

"It's my nickname," Toby broke in hastily. "Star's a funny name—I mean funny-peculiar."

"Oh, that—" The girl laughed. "I have a twin sister, and when Daddy first saw us he said we were no more alike than port and starboard, and the names stuck."

"Where's Port?" Toby always had to know everything and at once.

"In Warm Springs. She's never even seen Kewanaka. You see she had polio before we moved here from New Jersey."

"How awful!" exclaimed Nora.

"She's going to be perfectly all right," Star assured her. "Mother's with her now and is going to bring her home for Christmas."

"Mr. Thurston reminds me a little of your father," Ted told Nora. "The same cut of the jib."

"The bookish type, no doubt." Mark laughed.

Star laughed too. "I know your father's a publisher. In fact I've heard a lot about all of you from Mrs. Snow. That's why, when I heard you were on this train, I came in here hoping to meet you. When we were getting our house settled last fall, we had most of our meals at the Fo'c's'le."

15

"And ain't they sumpin'!" Toby's mouth watered at the thought. Then he leaned forward. "What did she tell you about us?"

"Well, for one thing, she told me that *you* ask a lot of questions."

"That's my intellectual curiosity," said Toby, loftily.

"Mrs. Snow took us out to the shed and showed us *Scud*," Star went on. "We have a sloop too—somewhat smaller than yours, though it's the same color—white with green decks. But it hasn't a cabin, and oh, how I wish it had. You see, when we lived on the Jersey coast, Port and I would just sail off until we found a nice private spot and go ashore and camp. But Mother says that sort of thing will be too rugged for her next summer."

"Mark made a model of *Scud*." Toby pointed to the rack. "It's up there."

"A model? Gosh, this I want to see!" exclaimed Ted.

"So do I," Nora confessed. "Toby and I haven't seen it since he finished it and we've never seen the glass case he made for it." She threw an appealing look in Mark's direction. "I made Toby promise not to coax you to show it to us until we got there, but—"

"Okay." Mark ran a hand over his dark brush of hair and nudged Toby. "Get up, twirp. I'll have to stand on the seat to get at it. I'll hand it down to you, Ted. Treat it gently."

And in a moment Mark was sitting in Toby's place, untying knots and laying back brown paper and quantities of corrugated cardboard.

"My gosh, man, that's a work of art!" Ted Chase's voice was almost hushed as the model emerged from its wrappings.

"That's as fine a ship model as ever I've seen." Mr. O'Brien was standing in the aisle now, and others were crowding around.

"It's all to scale—even the rigging." Toby explained. "He has to unwind thread and wire to get it just right."

"Where did you get those tiny brass cleats and those darling little anchors?" Pen had left her seat too.

"He made them himself." As Nora bent over to look, even her short fair curls seemed to bristle with pride.

"I wish I could find something besides paper for the sails." Mark was turning the glass case carefully around so they could view the model from all angles.

"The sails look grand to me." Mr. O'Brien had squatted down to see better. "Is the water she's sailin' in made of plaster?"

"He carved it—it's wood." Toby told him.

"Carved it? Did he now!" The big man was shaking his head. "An' the wind on the water just where it should be with yer boom out t' starboard that way."

"I can see the centerboard trunk!" Star was peering into the cabin, for Mark had made his model with the hatch-cover pushed back.

"It's all finished inside—even the cupboards and berths." Nora laughed. "Nobody will ever see them, but Mark wanted to make her for Father exactly as she was when we first saw her."

"She can only be about five or six inches, yet look at all that detail." Ted was peering down through the top of the case.

"Four inches, to be exact," Mark said, absently. He had been examining the plate glass case closely and now he looked across to Nora. "The real reason I almost missed the boat this afternoon was because I wasn't sure the cement I used to stick the glass together had dried thoroughly."

"Just give it time—it'll come unstuck just about the time your paper sails begin to wilt."

The Brices looked up to see who was talking. A boy with a sullen mouth was looking down at them through dark glasses.

Mark shrugged. "Could be you're right."

"Always the agin-er, aren't you, Joel?" Ted's nice grin was not in evidence now.

The boy grimaced and turned away.

"Who is that guy anyway?" Toby asked Ted.

"Joel Fleet— That's right, you didn't meet him last summer. He had a job over in Rocky Brook."

"Don't pay any attention to Joel," Star said. "He's a misan—well, I never can pronounce the word, but it means he has a perpetual hate on the world. He lives next door to us, and I find the best way to handle him when he's like this is to simply ignore him. He calls the *Mary Christmas* the floating wash tub." She gave a little laugh. "I must admit she is a beamy old lady at that."

"Is that the name of your sloop?" Toby asked her.

Star nodded. "Granny's name is Mary, and she gave her to us for Christmas. She's an old boat. She wasn't even new when we got her."

"Neither was ours when we got her," Toby said. "But Father always says it's not the age of a boat that matters most—it's how she's kept up."

"How big is the *Mary Christmas?*" Mark was carefully re-wrapping his model.

"Eighteen feet overall with six foot beam." Star laughed again. "That's why Joel calls her a wash tub."

"*Scud's* beamy too," said Nora, "but that makes her comfortable to live in."

"OW!" Toby, who was stooped over in the aisle, straightened up and began to alternately rub and blow on the knuckles of his right hand.

"What happened, Toby?" Nora started to her feet, but the train jolted and she abruptly sat down again.

"I was just picking up a folder of book matches, and that jerk in the dark glasses stepped on my hand. He did it on purpose too."

The matches happen to belong to me." The boy in the dark glasses bent over, and picking up the folder, looked at it closely before dropping it in the pocket of his red-and-black plaid mackinaw.

"You could have said so, couldn't you? *I* quit collecting the things for myself years ago. I just pick them up for Flo—for a kid I know." Toby looked up at the boy, contemptuously. "If you didn't wear glasses, I'd take a poke at you even if you are twice my size."

"Go on, Tobe!" a voice shrilled. "I'll help you clobber him!"

"You two and whose army?" The boy removed his glasses.

"Now, we'll have none of that on my train." Mr. O'Brien's hand shot out and grasped the collar of a boy about Toby's age who was threading his way among those who were standing in the aisle. "Go back to Charley, Spike Adams, and sit down. As fer you, Joel Fleet, mind yer manners. You know there's a rule against brawlin' on the train."

"There's a rule against dogs riding in the coaches too." Joel Fleet jerked a thumb toward Dinghy, who, having heard Toby's yelp of pain, had emerged from his hiding place. His tongue was lolling pathetically, as though he knew that he had done wrong, but his stick of a tail was wagging furiously to show that he expected to be forgiven.

As Joel Fleet raised his head and smiled insolently up at Mr. O'Brien, Toby's mouth dropped open. The boy's eyes were mere slits and his eyelids smooth and unwrinkled. In order to see the conductor's face, he had to throw his head back as far as it would go.

"A dog?" Mr. O'Brien leaned over and peered at Dinghy as though the little animal were much too tiny to be seen from his great height. "Why, so it is now!" Picking up the ball of jet-black fur, he tossed it in the air, caught it and tossed it up again, while Dinghy yelped and quivered with delight. "What a fierce little runt it is," he said, handing him back to Mark. Then turning to Joel, he shook a thick finger under his nose and roared, "*Cave canem, me boy, cave canem!*" and gave his hearty laugh. However, he stopped to clap Joel on the shoulder as he made his way along the aisle shouting, "Captain's Cove! Next stop, Captain's Cove!" He paused alongside the woman with the numerous packages. "Your station, Mrs. Beasley. I'll give ye a hand with yer Christmas shoppin'."

"Thank you, Mr. O'Brien." The woman smiled up at him as she handed him some of her parcels.

"What's the matter with that guy?" Toby had followed Mr. O'Brien out onto the platform.

"Eh?—Oh, Joel. Well, fer one thing the boy has no father."

"We have no mother, but that doesn't make us act like stinkers. What makes his eyes so funny?"

"He was born that way. A sunnier wee laddie you never saw till he began t' realize he was not like the other boys an' girls."

"Well, gosh, there's a kid in my class whose legs have been completely paralyzed most of his life. The high school boys have to carry him up and down stairs, but that doesn't make him act smelly, either."

"It's a bit different with Joel, I expect. Dr. Adams says he could have some operations that might make his eyes as good as yours, but his grandpa don't hold with such. So the way things is, Joel wouldn't be happy if he was on his way t' heaven with his shirt-tail full of red apples."

"But—"

"Get along in with ye an' let Mrs. Beasley through." Mr. O'Brien motioned with his head. "This is no night fer ye t' be outside in a thin little sweater."

When Toby got back to the others, Mark had out his sketch pad and pencil which were never far away from him, and now Star was perched on the arm of his seat.

"Yes," she was saying, eagerly, "that looks like the *Mary Christmas*. Do you really think she might be big enough to have a cabin built on her?"

Mark did some figuring at the side of the page, then nodded his head. "It could be done. I once saw plans in *Yachting* of a catboat with a cabin on her. She was a bit beamier than your sloop, but no longer." He started a sketch of a cabin interior below that of the sloop. "As I see it, there's room for berths on either side of the center-board trunk and maybe some to spare for narrow—er—

22

sort of catwalks. And if the seats were ripped out, you could have lockers in the cockpit for stowing stuff, the same as we have."

"Could I have that to show Daddy?" Star held out her hand.

"Gosh, not so fast!" Mark flipped the cover over the sketches and stowed the pad in his inside pocket. "I'd have to really see the boat first and take measurements to be sure it could be done."

"Ha!" Joel Fleet had been watching and listening quietly enough until now. "I once read about a guy who built a cabin on a boat that wasn't designed for one, and every time he stepped aboard, she'd buck him into the drink. He made money on it though—sold tickets for a quarter and offered ten bucks to anyone who could keep it afloat, and nobody could."

"Nuts!" Toby scowled at him. "If Mark says a cabin can be built on the *Mary Christmas*, it can."

"Just because he made that toy boat with the paper sails?" Joel was obviously enjoying himself.

"It's not a toy boat." Toby's chin jutted. "Mark's going to be a marine architect. Last summer he worked for Mr. Gardiner, and you ought to know he's the best yacht designer on the Island."

"He must have learned a lot, emptying trash baskets and sharpening pencils."

"You know so much!" Toby's eyes blazed. "The summer before last at camp, Mark designed and built a sailing dinghy, and he and Nora won practically all the races in it."

"Pipe down, Tobe," Mark said. "He's just trying to get

23

you to flip your lid. Besides, half the camp helped build *Driftwood*."

"Speaking of sailing dinghies," said Charley Adams. "Have you got your Sandpiper tuned up for the Christmas week regatta yet, Joel?"

"Yop. I'm going to put her over in the cove tomorrow and try her out, since the rain seems to have stopped for good."

"Sailing in December?" Toby looked blank.

"Haven't you ever heard of frostbite races?" Joel turned his dark glasses on Toby.

"I have," Mark cut in, quickly. "This is our first winter here. Out in Wisconsin where we come from, we're more used to iceboat races this time of year." He grinned. "I wish we had a Sandpiper. I'd like to race you while you're trying yours out."

"How about you and Nora borrowing ours?" Ted suggested. "She's all tuned up and ready to go too."

"The *Nipper?*" exclaimed Mark. "Your father's pride and joy?"

"He'll get a nudge out of you racing her—especially if you win."

"Well, gosh—swell. How about it, Fleet?" Mark looked up at the dark glasses.

"It's okay by me. Want to crew for me, Pen?" Joel asked.

Pen hesitated. "When?" she asked, slowly.

"Tomorrow's Saturday. How about then?"

"Well—all right. But it will have to be in the morning. I'm helping with the Christmas pageant at church, and there's a rehearsal in the afternoon." Pen spoke with such obvious reluctance that Joel said to Mark:

"Have you ever raced around here, Brice?"

Mark nodded. "Last summer we did some crewing."

"Do you know Captain's Cove?"

"We've been in there." Mark grinned at Nora and added, "I remember where the sand bar is. We almost got hung up on it once."

Joel thought for a moment, then shrugged. "Maybe you'd rather take on Pen. I'd just as soon take a chance on what's-her-name." He gestured toward Nora.

"Honora to you," Toby muttered, darkly.

"Okay," Pen agreed. "If it's all right with you, Nora."

Nora glanced up at Joel and almost surprised a smile on his sullen mouth. "I'd love to," she said. "I never dreamed we'd be sailing again until summer."

"Tomorrow's my day off." Mr. O'Brien had been listening too. "So, I'll be on hand in the *Monica* t' fish out the casualties."

"There'd better not be any." Pen shivered.

"Is this a private dog fight or can anyone get into it?" Charley Adams said.

Joel lifted his shoulders. "I wasn't figuring on a formal race—just out to the farthest buoy and back a couple of times, maybe. But the more the merrier."

CHAPTER 3

Kewanaka Bay! Next stop Kewanaka!"

Mark and Nora crowded into the aisle with the other passengers for Kewanaka Bay who were pushing those ahead of them as though fearful of being left aboard when the train pulled out. Toby had already gone to the baggage car.

"I'm glad the rain has stopped," Nora said over her shoulder to Ted. "But I hope we'll be able to get a taxi just the same. We've so much stuff."

"Don't worry. Someone's bound to give you a lift." Ted looked at her as though he knew something that she did not.

Toby, carrying his skis and dragging his duffel bag behind him, was the first to alight with Dinghy hopping along after him. Ted was carrying Mark's luggage, and Nora was carrying the model. Mark was taking care of everything else. The first person Toby saw when he hit the ground was an old friend.

"Hi, Mrs. Snow!" he called out, racing toward her as fast as his awkward skis and heavy bag would let him. "Did you walk all the way just to meet us?"

"Hello, Toby. My land, everything about you has grown except your hair—and Dinghy, of course." Mrs. Snow stooped to pat the little dog.

"You know what, Mrs. Snow?" Toby was looking at her, his head cocked to one side. "Come to think of it, you sort of remind me of *Scud*."

As Mrs. Snow straightened up, she looked very smart, standing under the station light in her blue transparent raincoat with the hat that matched framing her gray hair. Her scarlet storm boots made a pleasant spot of color on the drab platform. But there was a puzzled look on her face as she said, "*I* remind you of *Scud?*"

"I was telling Star Thurston on the train that Father says it's not *Scud's* age that matters most—it's how she's kept up. Look—I've got to grab a taxi before they're both taken."

"Hold on!" Mrs. Snow reached out to stop him. "I've

27

taken care of that." She looked down at him obliquely. "I'll have to think some about what you just said, before I decide whether or not it's a compliment."

"Mrs. Snow!" Nora and Mark were converging on her now.

"How are we going to get to the Fo'c's'le with all this duffel?" Mark was looking for a dry place where he could put some of it down.

Mrs. Snow touched his arm and pointed. "Look over there. No, *there*—in the parking space. See that station wagon? It's mine."

"Holy grommet!" Toby started toward it. "Can you drive it, Mrs. Snow?"

"Indeed I can. How I've lived all these years without a car, I don't know. Well, it's never too late for anything if you set your mind to it, I always say."

Ted laughed. "I told you not to worry about transportation, Nora."

"You people get in—you too, Ted," Mrs. Snow said. "I'll look around and see if anyone else is going our way."

"Oh, my gosh!" Mark gasped as they approached the station wagon. "What's its vintage? Can it really run?"

"It goes," Ted told him. "I've seen Mrs. Snow bouncing around in it with one of the guys from the garage. She took her driving test yesterday."

"You mean this is the first day she's driven alone?" Mark almost croaked. "Oh, gosh, I'd better take the model and go on foot." He had not liked that word "bouncing."

"Mrs. Snow might be hurt," Nora said. "I'll sit in the front seat where it's less bouncy and hold it on my lap."

"Well, what do you think of her?" Mrs. Snow was beaming on her first car. "I found two more passengers.

28

Star—you get in front with Nora and me, but let Joel in first. Mind the skis, Joel!"

"Joel Fleet?" Toby exploded from the back seat.

"You and Dink change places with me." Mark was crawling over the luggage. "And don't goof off. Joel may be a friend of Mrs. Snow's."

"That creep?" But Toby lowered his voice as he went forward to sit on the short seat alongside Ted, and let Joel squeeze past him.

"Everybody set?" Mrs. Snow got in behind the wheel.

"Okay back here," Joel sang out.

Mrs. Snow drew a deep breath and stepped on the starter.

"Whirrrr—whirrrr—whirrrr—"

"That's funny," she murmured. "It's always started right off before." Her foot came down on the starter again.

"Whirrrr—whirrrr—whirrrr—"

"Maybe we'd better get out and walk," said Mark, hopefully. But Ted was leaning over Mrs. Snow's shoulder and turning the ignition key.

"Try it again," he advised.

Again Mrs. Snow stepped on the starter.

"Whirr—ZOOM!"

"Yippee!" Toby shouted as the car shot out into the middle of the road with a grinding of gears.

"Better get over on your own side," Ted warned a moment later. "We're coming to a curve."

"That's right." Mrs. Snow laughed. "I keep forgetting other people might be on the road too." She jerked the wheel, and the car veered sharply to the right, then straightened out again with a whining of tires.

"This is terrific!" Toby broke into an old sea chanty, improvising some new words to suit the occasion, just as sailors always have done.

> "Rolling home, rolling home,
> Rolling home beside the sea.
> Rolling home in time for Christmas,
> Mrs. Snow to be with thee."

Mrs. Snow laughed. "I liked that, Toby, even if it was off key. I thought Nora was the only poet of the family."

"I'll write it down and autograph it for you," said Toby, grandly.

"Don't speak to the driver," Mark growled from the back seat. His eyes were closed, but they were painting pictures of the complete wreck of all those hours of painstaking care.

It was not many minutes before the ancient car jerked to a stop, but those minutes had seemed like hours to him.

"Okay, Star. Here's where you and Joel get off," Mrs. Snow was saying, when Mark opened his eyes.

They had stopped in front of a low white house whose windows were dark.

"Daddy must still be at his meeting," Star said. Then she leaned across Nora. "Mrs. Snow, would Mark have time to come to the carriage house and look over the *Mary Christmas?*"

"He thinks maybe a cabin could be built on her," Toby explained, "so that Port could go sailing next summer too."

"Really? A cabin on that little boat?" Mrs. Snow put the car in low gear. "Let's all go over and see it."

"Just where are we?" Toby asked, after Mrs. Snow had turned into a driveway. "I didn't notice which way we were going."

"That's Joel's house." Mrs. Snow pointed with her chin to a large shadowy house from whose lower windows yellow light was streaming. "The carriage house is out back —and Captain's Cove is down below it," she added, braking the car alongside another large dim building.

Mark took the model from Nora when he got out, and she let the others go on ahead while she stood for a moment, sniffing the wind blowing in off the Sound. It was a delicious smell—a combination of fish and salt water with a trace of pine and other scents she could not identify.

Ted and Joel were tugging at the big double doors of the carriage house when she caught up with the others. From here one could almost fling a stone into the cove. Nora stood apart for another brief moment, watching the inky meeting of sea and sky, and listening to the night sounds. The lapping of little waves on the beach and the patter of raindrops when a breeze shook the branches of the winter trees made a soft refrain. Then a sudden gush of light from the opened doors made her blink a little and she followed the others inside.

Toby whistled for Dinghy, who had gone off exploring, then pulled the doors together after he had reappeared.

"What a wonderful place for a party!" Nora exclaimed, looking around.

Mrs. Snow nodded. "In the old days—before the yacht club—Fleet's carriage house was the favorite social center of the town. In fact, before he died, Joel's father and mother gave many parties in here. But they built a garage on the house, so now it's only used wintertimes by Joel when he's working on his dinghy, and his grandfather lets the Thurstons keep their sloop here."

At first Mark was too preoccupied, gently shaking his model and listening for tell-tale rattles to notice much, but satisfied at last that it had survived its rough passage, he began to look around.

At one end of the barn-like room, was a stone fireplace, and at the other, an old pot-bellied stove. Despite the fact that there were two boats sitting in chocks on either side of the stove, there was enough room left over in which to give a barn dance. Ted was running his hand over one of the boats and saying:

"You've done a sweet job on her, Joel. She ought to be faster than ever. You'll have to be good, Mark, to keep the *Nipper* between her and the finish line tomorrow."

"Are they racing tomorrow?" Mrs. Snow asked.

Nora explained about the race, and that Mr. O'Brien was towing the *Nipper* around to the cove early in the morning, and that the *Monica* was going to stand by as the rescue boat.

Mark walked over for a look at the dinghy. *"Fleetsark,"*

he murmured, reading the name on the stern. *"Fleetsark,"* he repeated, his forehead puckering.

"That was the name of my father's boat," Joel said.

"Now I have it!" Mark's eyes widened. "I read about her in *Cruising*. She was a ketch, wasn't she? And Fleet—I mean your father—sailed her to Greece."

"Yeah." Joel shrugged, indifferently. "She was a thirty-seven footer."

"All the way to Greece?" exclaimed Toby, who had been absorbed in examining an outboard motor that was racked up on the wall beside the dinghy, but now he was listening.

"It was a sort of gag." Joel still sounded indifferent. "My father went to Cornell, and that's in Ithaca, so he and a couple of other guys sailed her to Ithaca, Greece."

"That's a fur piece for a gag," remarked Toby. "Say! do you still have the charts they used?"

"Yes. Why?"

"Well, I'm collecting charts of important voyages. I have a couple of really valuable ones, and Father's trying to get me some that were used in famous Bermuda races. You see he's publishing a book about—" Toby stopped short and then went on, "But, of course, you wouldn't want to trade any of yours with me."

"How right you are." Joel snickered, then said to Mark, "What do you think of the wash tub?" and nodded toward the other boat.

Mark walked over to it, and Star looked as though she were holding her breath while he looked it over. Finally, without saying a word, he set his model on one of the seats, and climbing into the boat, measured the cockpit with his eyes. Then he looked up. "Is there a tape measure or ruler of some kind handy?"

"Daddy has a steel tape in his tool kit in the house." Star started for the door.

"Don't bother, Star." Mrs. Snow began to search through her handbag. "I always carry one with me, because there always seems to be something to measure for the Fo'c's'le." She found it and handed it to Mark.

They all watched in silence while he took measurements which he jotted down on his sketch pad.

"It could be done, just as I thought," he said at last. "There's plenty of room for pipe berths on either side of the centerboard trunk, and that would leave you a fair-sized cockpit too."

"And to get headroom in the cabin, you'd only have to move up the gooseneck on the mast and refit sail." Joel grinned, mockingly. "Easy—if you're a sailmaker."

Mark glanced down at the mast and boom chocked up alongside the boat. "Just as she is, I'm sure you could put a cabin on her the boom would clear. But, even so, if I were designing a cabin for her, I'd lower the floorboards in the cabin part and build watertight bulkheads between it and the cockpit. That way the cabin could be built lower and not stick up like a sore thumb. Of course there'd only be sitting-up headroom, but that's all we have in ours."

"What would you make the cabin of?" Star asked.

"Well, to do it right, I think the sheathing should be of mahogany—"

"Canvas covered on top to match the decks." Mrs. Snow nodded, knowingly.

"And the framing and trim should be of oak," Mark went on.

"What? No teak?" Joel threw back his head and silently went through the motions of loud guffawing. "Have you any idea what all that would cost? Smalltown school teachers and principals aren't exactly loaded with what it takes."

"Oh, I don't know—" Ted looked thoughtful. "The materials shouldn't cost too much. I'll bet now that the shipyard has stopped taking orders for new yachts, there's lots of stuff lying around you could maybe buy almost for free."

"Corbey's yard has stopped building yachts?" exclaimed Toby.

"A lot of the big yards have," Ted explained, and added, "High cost of U.S. labor and cheap foreign competition."

"Who would build your cabin?" Mrs. Snow asked Star.

"I thought Daddy might, and I could help. He has every kind of tool imaginable and is good with them. It might take us the rest of the winter, but that wouldn't matter."

Mrs. Snow pursed her lips and shook her head. "I really don't think you should ask him to, Star. He needs every extra minute he can get working on that Ph.D."

"That's right." Star's face fell.

"How about you, Mark? You could build it, couldn't you?" Toby said. "I'd help. We haven't anything much else to do. Maybe we could start it now, anyway, and finish it during the spring vacation."

"You've got an idea, Tobe!" Ted walked over to Mark. "If you designed the cabin and bossed the job, and the gang pitched in and helped, we might even get it done by the time Port gets home."

"That's a grand idea," said Nora. "I'm rather handy with a palm and needle. I could sew the canvas for the pipe berths."

"And I'll swat the grommets in!" Toby cried. "We have a mallet and die."

"And when you need advice," Joel put in, "I can always give you from two to two-two some Tuesday."

"Excruciatingly humorous!" Toby made a gagging sound.

Joel thrust his hands into the pockets of his bright plaid mackinaw and swaggered toward the doors, just as they cracked open, and a man slipped through.

"Good evening, Ferd," Mrs. Snow greeted him.

The man grunted and barely touched the rim of a brown felt hat that, Nora decided, would have slipped down over his long nose if it were not for his big ears holding it up. "The Mad Hatter!" she giggled to herself.

"You didn't tell the old man you weren't coming back on the school bus," the man whined nasally to Joel.

"So what?"

"So, I've been looking all over town for you."

"What for?"

"Your old lady's taking you to the Valley to collect the rents is what for."

Joel jerked his hands out of his pockets and started for the man. "Don't you call my mother that!"

"Okay, okay—" The man shrank away and his nasal whine became a bleat. "She—I mean *Mrs. Fleet*—is waiting outside in the car for you!"

"What's the idea?" Joel pushed past him. "Why aren't you collecting as usual?"

"Because—" The man hesitated. "Because the old coot

has a bee in his bonnet about something. He wants me to help at the gas station Friday nights, and until he can find someone else to collect the rents for him, you're it."

"Oh, dear!" Mrs. Snow exclaimed. "Your mother hates going to the Valley—especially at night."

"Whose gonna drive him then?" The man pointed his long nose in Mrs. Snow's direction. "He ain't got a driver's license yet that I know of."

Joel, his face very red, banged the doors open, and the man followed him out.

"What was that all about?" Toby grinned. "Boy, is Joel ever hacked!"

"That Ferd Snively!" Mrs. Snow's lips narrowed. "All bleat and no chin! Poor Ida May—she's scared of her own shadow, and the Valley is the one unsavory spot in town. They have to collect the rents on pay day there before the men drink up the money."

"I feel sorry for Mrs. Fleet," Star said, "but it serves Joel right having to do something for his grandfather. I know he's sort of crabby, but Joel doesn't have to be quite so disrespectful to him."

"Joel!" Mrs. Snow sighed. "If only his father had lived—"

"What's all that stuff about his grandfather not letting Spike's father operate on his eyes so he won't look so goofy?" Toby asked. "Mr. O'Brien was telling me. Can't they afford it?"

Mrs. Snow smiled wryly. "Old Mr. Fleet is probably the warmest native in these parts."

"That means he's rich," Ted translated. "He owns property all over the place, but he's a stubborn, sot, Long Island Yankee. Gosh, my dad told me that back in the depression when all the banks closed, he swore he'd never trust another dollar of his to a bank again, and they say he never has."

"Where does he keep his wampum then?" asked Toby.

Ted grinned. "There've been rumors that he buries it— the old pirate blood coming out in him. Haven't you read about the pirate, Captain Fleet, in that book Mrs. Snow has? Captain's Cove is supposed to be named for him."

"You hush, Ted!" But Mrs. Snow laughed. "Fleet's not an uncommon name around here. Just because he sometimes acts like a pirate doesn't mean a thing. There are better things you can do while you're here, Toby, than to hunt for buried treasure." Her eyes twinkled. "Besides, the ground's too hard with frost for digging."

"But what was that about an operation on Joel's eyes?" Nora had gone over to close the doors that Joel had left creaking in the wind.

"That's just another one of old Mr. Fleet's sot ideas," Mrs. Snow said. "Since Joel's father died having his appendix out, he's been dead set against hospitals and operations. Though the truth is that if he'd let the doctor take his son to the hospital sooner, they could have saved his life."

"But can't his mother do something about Joel's eyes?" Nora asked.

Mrs. Snow shook her head. "Not Ida May. She can't face up to anything, and old Mr. Fleet terrifies her."

"Well, even so, Joel needn't take it out on the world," Toby said. "He's apt to get dangerous. I read about a guy who only had one droopy eye, and he looked so sinister, he started to act that way when he was just a kid. After he came out of reform school, he said to his father, 'Pappy, from now on out, I'm going to live by the gun.' And that's just what he did. He hitch-hiked a ride with a family that had four little children and made them take him across the desert. Then he killed them all and dumped their bodies—"

"Toby, you ghoul! You're making it all up!"

"No, I'm not, Nora. Honest. I read it in one of those True Crime Story magazines—and as soon as I saw Joel's eyes—"

"True Crime Stories! If Father knew—"

"Land sakes!" Mrs. Snow looked at her wristwatch and tactfully cut off whatever Nora was going to say. "We'll never have supper tonight if we don't get back to the house. You must be starved, Toby."

"He can't be." Nora was feeling in her coat pockets. "When did you filch those candy bars I had?" She looked at Toby, accusingly.

"When you were mooning at the moon that wasn't there. It is now, though." Toby had his nose glued to one of the windows. "And stars too—lots of them! It'll be clear for the race tomorrow."

"What about the cabin, Mark?" Star said. "Do you think— You know, what Ted suggested—that if we all helped—"

Mark had only been half-listening to the others. He had been thinking that designing and building a cabin on the boat would certainly add to his experience, but now he broke in doubtfully. "Maybe the lumber and stuff might run pretty high."

"Why don't you ask your father what he thinks, Star?" Toby suggested. "He's home now—or anyway there are lights on in your house."

"You stay and explain things to him, Mark." Mrs. Snow

started for the door. "It'll be some time before supper, and I can come back and get you."

"You don't need to do that, Mrs. Snow," Star said, eagerly. "Daddy will be glad to run him around in the car."

"I'll go along with you, Mrs. Snow, and help with supper." Nora pushed the doors open.

"That will be fine. We'll leave the men to their more important affairs. I'm sure your father won't mind dropping Ted off too, Star, since he lives so near us." Mrs. Snow started to follow Nora, then remembered something. "I almost forgot, Star. On the way to the station, I left some supper for you folks in the icebox. I knew you'd be late after the game, and probably too hungry to throw a good hot meal together. Just pop the pan in a moderate oven for about half an hour. There's an apple pie on the table for dessert."

"What's in the pan?" asked Toby.

"Flounders stuffed with shrimp—one of Mrs. Fleet's recipes. She can fuss up a common fish fit for a banquet."

Star shook her head after Mrs. Snow had closed the doors behind her. "Isn't she something? Just like a pioneer neighbor."

"But she cooks better food," said Toby. "I hope we're having the same thing you are."

CHAPTER 4

NORA COULD SMELL the fog—salty and damp—even before she opened her eyes in the gray dawn of Saturday morning. When she looked at her windows, they seemed to have been curtained outside with thick gray gauze. She closed her eyes again and smiled a little, remembering what she had been dreaming—that they had built a cabin on the *Mary Christmas* with a galley quite as big as Mrs. Snow's kitchen. She wondered what the cabin really would be like now that Mr. Thurston had given them the green light. He sounded nice—and Mark said, quite as interested in the project as Star. She started to doze off again when a sea gull's scream, cutting through the deep silence of early morning, startled her to complete wakefulness. She reached for her warm robe, lying across the foot of the bed, then swinging her legs over the side, slid her feet into her woolly slippers. As she listened to the brr-ooomph of the foghorn on the lighthouse, she was reminded that this was the morning of the race and that the first one up was to wake the others. Nevertheless she knelt for a moment at the low east window, breathing in the salt air, and looking out to a paling sky where a last little star winked briefly at her through the fog. As she listened to the squealing gulls, and to the busy twittering of smaller birds waking up in the rustling pine tree below the window,

41

Santa Clara County Free Library

she murmured, "'Earth with her thousand voices praises God.'" Shivering a little now, she closed the window and got to her feet.

Early as it was when they crept downstairs, Mrs. Snow had been up long before them.

"We're having breakfast in front of the living room fire," she called out to them from the kitchen. "The furnace hasn't had a chance to really come up yet. Come on, Dink. I have something for you out here."

"You shouldn't have bothered to get breakfast for us," Nora protested. "I was going to rustle up something or other."

"Nonsense!" Mrs. Snow came into the hall, carrying a laden tray which she handed to Mark. "You have to be warmly lined for winter sailing, and I hope you're wearing your warmest clothes."

"I am." Toby was eyeing the telephone on the hall table. "I have on my ski longies under my jeans. May I make a phone call, Mrs. Snow?"

"If it's to Spike Adams, he phoned at the cracka—almost before I was downstairs—to say that their sister is crewing for Charley, and that Flossie's mother won't let her put her dinghy over until summer, because her idea of sailing seems to be more often under the water than on it."

"Oh, my gosh!" Toby thrust his hands into the pockets of his jeans. "I was going to skipper for her and I'd have kept us right side up."

"But I called Mr. O'Brien," Mrs. Snow went on, imperturbably, "and he says the three of you—and Dinghy, of course—can go along with him in the *Monica*, if you'd like."

"How about that!" Toby was smiling again. "You think of everything, Mrs. Snow. Do Spike and Flossie know?"

"Conor was going to call Spike so I could get on with breakfast."

"Did he say where I was to meet him?"

"He'll bring the *Monica* into the old wharf in the cove, and you'd better watch your step going out. A lot of the planking is rotten and full of holes."

"Gee, I wonder if Mr. O'Brien will let me take charge of the engine," Toby said.

"I wouldn't set my heart on it." Nora was following Mark into the living room to take charge of the contents of the tray.

Mrs. Snow had covered a bridge table with a white cloth, and there was a smaller table alongside her place. Since she had tutored Nora in the art of table-setting as well as cooking the summer before, Nora knew just what to do. After carrying the tray several times to the kitchen, then back again with covered dishes that she placed on the side table, she plumped down a steaming bowl of oatmeal at each place.

"Put another log on the fire, Mark," Mrs. Snow said, while Toby drew up the chairs.

The fire was flickering warmly, its reflection bright on the paneled wall over the fireplace and on the polished ceiling beams above it. But the rest of the room was full of shadows, as thick fog still shrouded the windows. The little wood-paneled living room had never looked cozier, but nobody was noticing that because, never before, even at the Fo'c's'le, had they sat down to such a breakfast.

43

Few words were spoken as the great quantities of country ham and scrambled eggs, hot muffins, cocoa and coffee that followed the oatmeal, disappeared with almost alarming rapidity.

Finally, "Umm," sighed Toby, blissfully, as he finished the last of his helping of apple pie. "Dessert for breakfast."

"There's more left." Mrs. Snow lifted the pie server invitingly.

"Well—just a small piece, then."

"Honestly, Toby, how can you!" Nora's mouth tightened.

"I'm a growing boy, remember."

"At the rate you're eating, you'll soon be growing the wrong way, *Tubby*." Mark folded his napkin and pushed back his chair. "I've got to get cracking and pronto. Joel may need help taking the dink down to the cove."

"He has a contraption with wheels he uses, but go along anyway—all of you." Mrs. Snow held up her hand, arrestingly, as Nora started to clear the table. "Leave the dishes where they are. I haven't much to do this morning."

"Well, all right," Nora said. "We've already made our beds."

"Good." Mrs. Snow stood up. "I'll run you down in the car."

"No thanks," Mark said, hastily. "We'll walk. It's all downhill."

Last night when they had gone into the shed to look *Scud* over, and he had seen the station wagon parked alongside her with only inches between them, he had begun to worry anew about Mrs. Snow's doubtful talent as a driver.

"Well, if you're sure—" Mrs. Snow sounded almost wistful. "You'd better wear your storm boots, then— Excuse me, Toby—your sea boots, as well as your oilskins. It's messy underfoot. Your things are still where you left them last summer."

When they trooped back to the hall, Mrs. Snow was standing in front of the living room fireplace. Last night Mark had moved some of the pewter mugs and tankards that were lined up on the mantel, and had placed his model there. Now Mrs. Snow was looking at it.

"I declare it's really beautiful, Mark," she said. "I can't keep my eyes off it."

"I feel that way too," said Nora. "But we'll have to hide it soon. You know how unexpectedly Father pops out to see us when we're here."

"I'll put it away this very morning." Mrs. Snow turned around, then burst out laughing. "You look like ads for codliver oil," she said.

Toby looked at himself in the hall mirror. "We do, at that! So, if you'll dip into your deep freeze and find us a trio of codfish, Mrs. Snow, we'll sling them over our shoulders and be on our way."

Mrs. Snow stood in the open doorway, hugging herself against the damp cold, as she watched them go down the porch steps. "Maybe I'll have my after breakfast cuppa with Ida May Fleet, so likely I'll be seeing some of the race from her kitchen windows."

"How good is Joel at racing?" Toby asked her.

"Plenty good. I heard that, when he was in Rocky Brook last summer, he won lots of races."

"Humph!" Toby lifted his shoulders. "That Rocky

Brook crowd! When they come over here, they're not so hot."

Early as it was when they reached the carriage house, Joel must have been there before them, for his dinghy was gone.

As they made their way through the half-frozen puddles down the path toward the water, Nora looked up at the dripping trees that lined it, but they had lost their heads in the mist. She had the feeling of being in a dark, clammy cave.

> "Where Alph the sacred river ran
> Through caverns, measureless to man,
> Down to a sunless sea—"

she recited, her boots squelching in rhythm through the puddles.

However, a fitful wind, blowing in from the sea, had torn great holes in the fog drifting over the pewter water in the cove, and there were only a few wisps of it over the Sound.

"That must be *Fleetsark* out there." Toby stopped on the beach, and the others stopped too, for a moment, to watch a little white-winged dinghy tacking toward the wharf.

"It is," Mark said. "At least, I'm quite sure there can't be two plaid mackinaws like that in Kewanaka."

Just then Dinghy came tearing out of the sea grass and began to bark and scamper around in a circle, chasing his tail.

"That's the way he acts when he hears a powerboat," Toby said. "Listen."

"Chug—chug—chug—" A boat they could not see was heralding its approach.

"I'll bet that's the *Monica!*" Toby started to run.

"Kick off your boots and leave them on the wharf," Nora called after him. "We don't need them any more."

So Toby flung his down, and remembering Mrs. Snow's warning, picked his way cautiously along the rotting planks, with Dinghy under his arm.

"We won't be needing our oilskins either," Mark shouted.

It was the *Monica* they had heard. Mark and Toby stood on the end of the wharf and watched her slowly chugging her way into the cove, towing three dinghies. But Nora cautiously felt her way down the steps and dropped into *Fleetsark* which Joel held steady for her.

"I don't see *Nipper.*" Toby was waving to Spike and Flossie who were in the bow of the *Monica*, and at the same time was trying to identify the occupants of the dinghies. "There's Charley and Grace in the *Dither*, and that's Gus Armstrong—"

"Where are Ted and Pen?" Mark shouted when the fishing boat was in earshot.

"Ain't they here yet?" Mr. O'Brien boomed back. "They told us t' go on without them," he continued as he came alongside the wharf and tossed the dock line to Toby. "I don't know who's bringin' them around."

After Toby had made the line fast, he handed Dinghy down to Spike, then hit the deck of the fishing boat himself, just as Dinghy squirmed out of Spike's arms and dashed to the stern, his ears twitching. Toby listened and heard a faint throbbing sound which grew louder, and another boat came sweeping around the point into the cove.

"It's one of the workboats from the shipyard," Mr. O'Brien said.

"Towing *four* dinghies!" Flossie Henderson squealed. "This may turn out to be quite a race!" The bands on her teeth glistened.

"There's the *Nipper!*" cried Toby. "Ted's in her."

The man at the wheel of the workboat stood up as he brought her alongside the *Monica*, and roared in a deep voice, "*Ave piscator!*"

"It's Sam Corbey!" Toby yelled. "What did he say, Mr. O'Brien?"

"It's Latin fer Hi, fisherman. What are you doin' home

from school?" Mr. O'Brien leaned over to shake the young man's hand. "Did they send ye down?"

"Expel me? The captain of the freshman dinghy team?" Sam Corbey laughed. "My room-mate drove down for a wedding, and I bummed a ride." He looked up at the wharf where Mark was standing, his mouth open and one hand cupped behind his ear. "What's the matter with you?" he demanded. "Have you gone deaf?"

"I'm listening for the Harvard accent," said Mark.

"He'd better not practice it around me," Pen threatened as she climbed out of the workboat and dropped into *Nipper* which Ted had pulled up.

"Are you still his date?" Toby asked her.

"Am I, Sam?" Pen, not the least bit embarrassed, laughed.

"I haven't given much thought to the subject this morning," Sam answered her. "We've had more important things to consider."

"Gosh," Toby remarked. "Even though you are a freshman again, you're as big for your dungarees as when you were a senior, last year."

Sam ignored him. "Ted and I have appointed ourselves a race committee of two," he told the others. "I brought along a couple of marker buoys and a gun. What's the course, Joel?"

"Twice around the outside nun and back. The wind's right for a start to win'ard."

Sam squinted out to the nun and nodded. "Okay, I'll anchor the committee boat over there." He gestured. "You go out on this side, between it and the buoy, and back on the other side, leaving the nun to port. Get that? Pass it along. You all should know the racing rules by now."

"I boned up on them, last night," Mark said before dropping into the *Nipper*.

Now most of the little white-sailed dinghies were jockeying near the buoy end of the starting line, fighting for the windward position. The fitful breeze had steadied, and overhead large patches of blue, shot through with sunshine gave promise of a clear and almost balmy December day.

Mark kept out of the dog fight. After looking over the course, he had decided that it would be to their advantage to start on a starboard tack, nearer the committee boat, and Pen had agreed. For the first five minutes after the preparatory gun had gone off, he managed to keep the *Nipper* on the right side of the line.

"Trim her in, Pen," he was saying, when the starting gun went BANG, and they hit the line.

They were really footing as they worked her up to windward and approached the other boats which were spread out with little space between them. *Fleetsark* was leading. *Nipper* passed under the stern of number 24, forcing number 35, which was Charley's *Dither*, to go about. Then they were sailing beside *Fleetsark*, and for the moment, put the other boats out of their minds.

Mark jibed to make the red nun and rounded it to take second place, for now fleecy gray-white clouds were gamboling, like lazy sheep, across the sun, and the breeze was becoming puffy. Joel had taken full advantage of a puff to shoot ahead. Then another puff helped *Nipper* along, and they were side by side again, but with plenty of water between.

"He's sailing awfully close to the sand bar," Mark said to Pen.

Pen nodded. "Joel knows the cove as though it were marked with chalk. He's all right. There's more wind over there." She looked around. "But we're doing all right too."

The two boats made one complete lap of the course without any serious competition from the other boats, and this time, *Nipper* was in first place after they rounded the nun. But again a friendly puff sent *Fleetsark* to leeward of her and out in front, and Charley's *Dither* was coming up fast. Then for some time *Nipper* and *Fleetsark*, heeled over on the same tack, maintained the lead with *Dither* close on their sterns. Then Mark came up into the wind.

"I'm going to try to pass Joel to win'ard, and blanket him," he told Pen. "He's sailing so close to the sand bar he can't get away."

Pen nodded and expertly handled the sheet.

After Mark had time to look around and see that he was still safe from *Dither*, he glanced over at *Fleetsark* and almost stood up. "He's heading her straight for the sand bar," he yelled. "I thought you said he knew—"

"He's going over it!" Pen exclaimed. "See? Nora's pulling up the board!"

For a few seconds Mark held his breath. The idiot! What a fool thing to do at half-tide. . . . He heard the steady chug-chug of the *Monica*, and the thrumming of the committee boat's engine. Mr. O'Brien and Sam must have seen too. If *Fleetsark* grounded, Nora and Joel were bound to get a ducking. . . . Then he let out his breath. *Fleetsark* had crossed the bar. Her sails luffed briefly then picked up the wind again, and Joel headed her straight for the finish line.

While Mark's attention was being distracted by *Fleetsark*, Charley, who was concentrating on the race, went through *Nipper's* lee to forge ahead of her. He waved and grinned, derisively, as he shot past. It was obvious that he felt sure of securing second place, at least.

Gritting his teeth, Mark put his mind back to sailing and took a hitch to westward to clear his wind.

Charley continued inshore, and that was his mistake. When the two boats converged again, Mark was in the weather berth.

BANG! Sam's gun went off as *Fleetsark* crossed the finish line with *Nipper* two seconds behind her, and *Dither* a close third.

52

"We bows to you, Marco!" Charley called out, as he came up into the wind to tack over to the wharf.

It was minutes before the other five dinghies straggled over the line.

As Mark and Pen drew near the wharf, Mark let out an exclamation. "Toby's flipped again. Look at him bawling out Joel!"

"I find Joel rather hard to take myself," Pen said.

Mark shrugged. "I know, but his mother seems to be a close friend of Mrs. Snow's, and to all intents and purposes, we're her guests while we're staying at the Fo'c's'le."

"What gives?" he asked, after they had come up into the wind beside the *Monica*.

"He cheated!" Toby was shouting.

"What do you mean 'cheated'?" Joel sneered back. "Nobody raised a protest, did they? And why? Because I didn't break a rule."

"Even Mr. O'Brien said he cheated," Toby told Mark.

"Now, Toby, yer kinda misquotin' me." Mr. O'Brien put a hand on Toby's shoulder. "What I said was—I thought crossin' the bar on purpose in December was kinda risky—t' say the least."

"Stow it, Tobe, you're off your course," Mark growled. "You're just burned up because there was no one to rescue."

"I like that!" Toby squealed. "You mean I wanted them to capsize and have Nora catch pneumonia? She could have, if they did."

"Listen, small fry," Joel said, wearily. "I've been over that sand bar at half-tide before. I warned her if she moved what could happen. And nothing did happen, did

53

it? Except that I won the race by a clever piece of strategy."

"Strategy!"

"Keep still, Toby!" Nora had seen that Mrs. Snow and another woman were gingerly making their way down the wharf toward them.

"Hi!" Mrs. Snow waved. "It was a good race."

"Good!" exclaimed Toby. "What was good about it? Just tell me, Mrs. Snow—what was good about it? Of all the rotten spo—"

Spike grabbed hold of Toby, and Flossie whispered something to him, while Mrs. Snow looked hard at him and said:

"This is Mrs. Fleet. She wanted to come out and meet Joel's new friends."

All the dinghies had crowded around, their grinning crews listening to the exchange between Toby and Joel, but now with sudden energy, they began to shake out sail bags and take off sail.

Even Toby greeted Mrs. Fleet politely. Quite suddenly he felt slightly deflated.

"Who's coming home with me?" Mrs. Snow asked, brightly, after the introductions had been made. "I've got the car here."

"I thought maybe Mark might like to go back to the yard with us," Sam said. "Pen and Ted have been telling me about the cabin for the Thurstons' boat, and I'm sure we could dig up the lumber for it, so they can get started right away."

"Where is Star, by the way?" Toby looked around. "I should have thought she'd have wanted to see the er-er-race."

Pen looked at him and laughed. "She helps at Haven Academy Saturday mornings, and while her mother's away, she has all the housework to do too."

"Haven Academy?"

"It's new since you were here, Toby," said Mrs. Snow. "It's a sort of boarding school for orphans and boys and girls from broken homes. They've taken the Avery estate on the top of Johnny Cake Hill, that's been empty so long."

"They're working on a shoestring, and are terribly under-staffed, so some of us try to help out when we can." Pen was transferring from the dinghy to the workboat.

"Let's get going." Ted dropped into the *Nipper* and pulled her up beside *Fleetsark*. "You coming too, Nora?"

Nora looked up at Mrs. Snow. "Can I help with dinner?"

"Mercy, no. You and Toby go along with the others. I'll pick up your boots and see that they get home. Dinner's at one, remember."

CHAPTER 5

Mark sat at the dinner table mechanically chewing the roast chicken and "all the trimmings" that Mrs. Snow had heaped on his plate, but he could just as well have been dutifully consuming parsnips and calf brains—both of which he detested. His thoughts were in a tangle.

After the race, Sam had scoured his father's shipyard and found the necessary lumber. Then he had left orders with one of the men in the shop to have it cut to Mark's measurements and delivered to the carriage house that day. After that he had borrowed the family car, and they had all gone to visit the ship chandler—who was Ted's father. And Ted, who had gone along with them, had helped them to collect cans of green and white paint, quantities of white lead, nails, screws, bolts and, among other things, a pair of small round port lights, because Mr. Chase had agreed with Toby that it would not look like a professional cabin without them. These purchases they had piled into the trunk of the car to take to the carriage house, where they had found Star and Mr. Thurston lining up tools for Mark's inspection.

There was no reason at all why they could not start working on the cabin that very afternoon, yet now a cold little lump was forming in Mark's stomach despite the good hot food he was packing into it. The only cabin he had ever actually built was the one on the model. Why had he let the others take for granted that he could do the job? He wondered if Joel's taunts might not have goaded him into wanting to show off. He shivered a little at the possibility. Then he remembered something Father had told him a long while ago. "Never be ashamed to admit that a snap decision might have been the wrong one," Father had said. . . . Was it too late to back out now? Maybe they hadn't started cutting the lumber at the shipyard yet. . . . He carefully laid down his knife and fork and, raising his eyes, looked out the window at the gulls soaring, dipping and swerving back and forth over the white-capped bay. And as he watched, something else Father had told him that day long ago, came back to him. "But on the other hand," he had said, "once you've made a well-thought-out decision that you think is right, stick to it." He took a deep breath, and the cold lump in his stomach began to melt. He knew that he had made a good plan for the cabin, and last night after supper, when he and Mr. Thurston were taking more accurate measurements, he had had the feeling that Mr. Thurston had thought so too. His hand went to the back pocket of his jeans where he had stowed his sketch pad, and as he watched a baby gull, sitting on a buoy, carefully raise its wings to follow its mother, he was sure that he, too, was ready to try his wings on the real thing.

"I said, where have you been, Marco Polo?" Nora was looking at him, curiously, from across the table. "You've been gone an awfully long time. Mrs. Snow has asked you three times if you want more chicken."

Mark looked down at his empty plate and shook his head. "No, thanks, Mrs. Snow. It—it was swell, though."

57

His lips twitched a little as he added to himself—"I think!"

"I'll get the ice cream then. You stay put, Mrs. Snow." Nora stood up and picked up her plate.

"What kind of ice cream?" Toby looked at Mrs. Snow.

"Banana."

"Oh, boy!"

Mrs. Snow turned to Mark. "What did Mr. Thurston say when he saw the lumber and hardware bills?"

Mark grinned. "He said it looked suspiciously like a give-away to him. But Sam and Ted told him they'd only given him a professional discount on the stuff. He didn't say anything more, but he sort of lifted an eyebrow as if he found that hard to believe."

Mrs. Snow nodded. "Everybody in town—especially those who have children—are crazy about Mr. Thurston. He's a wonderful change from poor old 'Fiddle-faddle' as the students used to call Mr. Fitell, the last principal."

"But he'll leave, won't he, to teach in a college or something when he gets that Ph.D.?" asked Toby.

Mrs. Snow shook her head. "That's what some folks are afraid of. But he was raised on the Island and has never been really happy away from it, so it's my guess he plans to stay here. Else why would he have bought his house from Mr. Fleet when he could have just rented it?"

"There are a few more things we'll have to get." Mark's mind was back on the cabin. "Pipe for the berths and canvas, for instance."

"I'm glad you reminded me, Mark." Mrs. Snow handed him his dessert. "You have enough canvas left over from making your tarp last summer to cover the cabin. And I have scads of green-and-white striped canvas—anyway enough for the berths if you don't think it would be too giddy."

"It will match the boat," said Nora.

They were the first to reach the carriage house, where they found that Mr. Thurston or Star had made a fire in the old stove which was already taking the chill off that end of the big, high-ceilinged room. Also, someone had improvised a workbench of boards stretched across sawhorses alongside the battered table where the tools and paint brushes were lined up.

Mark took off his windbreaker and stood for a moment warming his hands at the stove while he looked over the lumber stacked up alongside the purchases they had made at the ship chandler's. "The first thing we do," he said finally, "is to bust out the for'ard bulkhead. The foot of the port berth will have to extend under the forepeak if Star wants the shelf for her stove where we have ours." Going over to the table, he picked up a screw driver and pried open a can of green paint. "Your first job, Tobe, is to crawl under the forepeak after we knock out the bulkhead, and give it a coat of paint. So find a stick or something and start stirring."

Mark and Nora were still attacking the bulkhead when Star, who was in her working jeans too, staggered in with a scuttle full of coal.

"Thanks," she gasped, when Mark took it from her. "The coal bin's around at the side, and Daddy said to tell you we have plenty of logs if you think we need a fire in the fireplace. What can I do?"

"Nothing for the moment, but stick around." Mark grinned.

Toby had crawled into the forepeak with his can of green paint and brush where he was trying to accomplish the difficult task of getting more paint on the little boat than on himself, and the others had ripped out the seats and taken up the floor boards when Ted and Sam arrived.

"Nice to have you aboard!" Mark greeted them. "I see you remembered to bring your own tools. Did you mark them so they won't get mixed up with Mr. Thurston's and ours?"

Sam nodded. "I'll leave mine here in case you need extras."

Mark put Nora and the newcomers to work on the tedious job of lowering the floor board supports, and after he had seen they did not need him, he climbed out of the cockpit and left them to it. And when Flossie and Spike burst in, he started them sandpapering half-round trim under Star's direction. He was anxious to get at the job of cutting the ribs that were to be attached to the coaming. Once they were on, he could bolt in place the oak framing beams that had been cut on the bandsaw in the shipyard.

After that came the job of cutting down the coaming to make a fair curve where the cockpit and cabin met. He rather dreaded attempting what his developing eye for line insisted should be done.

Nora sensed his tension and stepped out of the boat to watch him, just as Mr. Thurston came over from the house to see what was going on.

"Better use the keyhole saw on the curve," he suggested, after Mark had scored in the cutting lines on the varnished surface with a sharp nail.

Mark started to make the first cut when the door opened, and Joel strolled in.

"Need any advice yet?" He stood close to Mark and a little behind him.

Again Mark attempted to make the first cut, but the palms of his hands, for some reason, became damp and he had to stop and rub them dry on his jeans. It was important that there be no slips on this particular job or all the careful measurements that he and Mr. Thurston had made the night before, would have to be changed.

Joel laughed softly. "How does it feel to be hacking away at somebody else's property?"

"Stop breathing down his neck," Mr. Thurston commanded, sharply. "Get back out of his way."

"That's right." Star had stopped work to watch too. "If you can't help, don't hinder!"

Grasping the coaming in one hand and gripping the saw with the other, Mark held his breath and made the first tentative cut. . . . Why the saw was cutting through that oak board like butter! Backward and forward—backward and forward the saw went while the others watched, saying nothing, except when Mark had rounded the corner and stopped. Then Mr. Thurston reminded him that he could use the ripsaw going with the grain.

As Nora watched Mr. Thurston light his pipe, she agreed with Ted that he was very like Father. She could tell he thought they were doing a good job without his having to say so.

By the time Toby was finished with his paint job, Pen had come from the rehearsal at church, a small boy following in her wake.

"Hi!" she exclaimed when Toby, pushing his paint can before him, crawled out from under the forepeak. "If it isn't the boy with the green hair!"

Toby started to put his hand up to feel, but thought better of it after noticing that it, too, had received a generous portion of green. He shrugged, philosophically. "It'll wear off. Hi, Benjie!" He had caught sight of the small boy. "How's my favorite sittee?"

The little boy looked at him solemnly. "I like man sitters best. I wish you lived here in the wintertime too."

"Well, of all the ungrateful imps!" exclaimed Pen. "Here

I've been taking care of him all afternoon and for free!"

"Can I help you paint?" the little boy asked Toby.

Toby shook his head. "I'm finished for now, but maybe some other time I'll let you help. Gosh, painting sure is thirst-making. I'm swallowing cotton. How about a grog break, Mark?"

"You treating?"

"Well, sure—that is I would only—"

"You left your money at the Fo'c's'le." Nora sniffed.

"I'll see what we have in the refrig." Star got up from the box she was sitting on, dusting off her sweater.

But Mark shook his head as he handed Toby a dollar bill. "No scrounging. Anyone who wants a drink can pay me. Since it was your idea, Tobe, you can leg it down to that store on Oak Lane. Make mine a coke."

"Mine too." Sam, as well as the others, was digging into his pockets for coins.

"Everybody want coke—you, Benjie?"

Benjie thought for a moment. "I haven't any money."

"That's all right, butch," Mark said. "You're our guest, today—yours is on the house."

Benjie thought that over too. "My mother doesn't allow me to have coke, but I can have ginger ale."

"Count me out," said Joel, strolling away as casually as he had strolled in.

"That's okay by me." Toby was shrugging on his pea jacket and counting noses. "One ale and nine grogs."

"Take my bike, Tobe," Spike called after him. "It's on the porch." He gestured toward the Thurstons' house.

"Why don't we lug over the porch swing and some chairs," suggested Star. "They're in the garage. We might as well be comfortable. I'd better get a bottle opener too."

"Toby has one on his scout knife," Nora told her.

By the time Toby came back with his cardboard carriers of bottles, the porch swing was creaking like a frog in front of the glowing stove, and porch chairs had been set up in the space that *Fleetsark* had occupied. When he was not working on his dinghy, Joel kept it in a shed near the beach.

"I'll be taker-back too, if you like," Toby said, casually, after he had opened the bottles, and Spike and Flossie were handing them around.

"You would!" Nora almost snorted. "In our family," she explained, "taker-back gets the deposit money."

"I'll help you take back, Toby!" Spike and Flossie cried, simultaneously.

"You can give me back the change from my dollar bill right now, twirp." Mark held out his hand. "One round nickel."

"How did the rehearsal go?" Ted asked Pen after he had taken a long swig of his drink.

"Oh, the way first rehearsals for the Christmas pageant usually go." Pen shrugged. "Everybody thinks they know the whole thing by heart from last year so not many showed up—including you, my fine, feathered friend!"

"We always had the same trouble when we were at boarding school," said Nora. "So last year we decided to make some changes."

"We always give exactly the same one year after year," Flossie said. "You know—the Christmas story with angels and shepherds and we-three-kings-of-orien-tar. Only I'm never in it because I can't carry a tune locked up in a suitcase," she added, smugly.

"We always had that one too," Toby put in. "But last

64

year Nora wrote a kind of curtain raiser for the pageant—the story of Saint Nicholas and the three little boys the innkeeper pickled in brine to make bacon."

"I know it sounds grue." Nora laughed. "But we made a sort of light operetta of it—with considerable help from the music department, I might add. However the best thing about last year's program was the way we staged it—the way they used to in medieval days on Christmas Eve. We had a platform built on a wagon and put the program on outdoors in the courtyard of the village church."

"Jeepers!" Spike shivered. "Didn't the angels freeze?"

Nora shook her head. "We only had a few of them on the stage, and they wore their ski things under their robes."

"They were pretty husky looking angels." ̶ laughed. "As far as I'm concerned, the best thing the whole show was its brevity. Most Christ̶ grams go on forever."

"People came from all over to see it, though," Toby said, "and they all brought gifts. The farm people brought hams and cheese and turkeys—all sorts of things. One farmer even brought a live pig. And at the end of the program, after the three kings had left their gifts, all the people marched up and laid theirs in front of the manger —only they were really for the Old People's Home. It was mildly stupendous."

"Because that made the people who brought things feel that they were part of the pageant too," Nora explained.

"Say!" The swing stopped creaking as Sam, who was sitting on it between Pen and Star, put his feet flat on the

65

floor. "Why couldn't we do something like that for Haven Academy? The whole town is interested in seeing them get along, and they need about everything imaginable—food, athletic equipment, books, toys for the children—"

"I wonder if we could!" Pen broke in. "Could you help us, Nora?"

Nora looked over at the boat. "We wouldn't want anything to interfere with getting the cabin finished before Christmas, but maybe we could rehearse some of the Saint Nicholas play right here. I guess I must have had a hunch because I packed it with my books. Mark was the innkeeper last year, and I was his wife, and Toby was one of the little boys. So since we already know those parts—"

"That was last year," interrupted Toby. "I was too old to be a little boy then and I'm much too old to be one now."

"Oh, Toby—you sing off key so beautifully! You see," Nora explained, "the other two little boys had beautiful voices, and Toby's made their songs really funny."

"I'll be one of the other little boys," Spike offered. "I sing like an angel."

"Who says?" demanded Toby.

"My grandmother. Do-re-me-fa-so—" Spike ran up the scale in a clear soprano. "You'd better catch me before my voice changes, Nora."

"But gosh," Toby protested, "you're a year older than I am, even if you are in the same grade."

"I may not be a Quiz Kid like you," Spike retorted, "but I sure sing sweet. Say, Nora, would it matter if the third little boy was a colored boy?"

"Of course it wouldn't. They aren't supposed to be

66

brothers. Their fathers sent them from the city to live in the country with Saint Nicholas to be tutored, and they lost their way."

"Swell. Harvey Monroe is one of the kids at Haven Academy. He's about my size and sings even sweeter than I do. Oh, gosh!" Spike's face fell. "Harvey doesn't go to our church. He goes to the one in Captain's Cove."

"Maybe the two churches could join in on the program," suggested Ted. "Both Mr. Winslow and Mr. Ogilvie take turns conducting vesper services at the academy Sunday nights."

"That's a good idea." Pen nodded. "Maybe they could supply the angels and we could supply the kings, for instance."

"Can I be one of the little boys?" Benjie piped up. "I'm going on six and I sing real good."

"You already have a part in the pageant," Pen said, quickly.

"But I'd rather rehearse here than in Sunday school." Benjie's lip quivered.

"I tell you what," Nora said. "You could rehearse both places. We had a little song for a very small child at the end of the program," she told the others. " 'And a Child Led Them.' It's the cue for the people to bring their gifts to the Christ Child. I haven't the music for that, but I know it."

Benjie was smiling as he finished his ginger ale.

"Look, Nora—" Toby was frowning. "Why can't we be just *boys*—why do we have to be *little* boys?"

"Because Saint Nicholas is the patron saint of *little* children—among other things."

"Such as?" Toby asked.

"Such as pawnbrokers." Mark grinned. "That's why they always have three gold balls over their shops."

"What's the Saint Nicholas part—tenor or bass or what?" Pen asked Nora.

"Bass—like Sam. Oh, Sam, you'd be a wonderful Saint Nicholas. He should be tall and dressed in a red robe and a high sort of bishop's miter to make him look even taller and he wears a white beard. If I wrote out the part for you tonight, could you learn it before you came home again? It's not very long."

"Gad! I sure got myself into something!" Sam laughed. "Okay. But someone will have to rig up the costume for me."

"Ted's mother and Mrs. Snow are great at that sort of thing," Pen said.

"Swell." Mark stood up. "Maybe they can rig up something for us too."

While they were talking, the sun had slipped down in the west, and now purple dusk filled the great room.

Mark went over and switched on the lights. "Come on, crew. Right now operation *Mary Christmas* is staring us in the face. I want to finish cutting down the coaming."

Pen leaned forward. "Listen, Mark. I know I haven't done a thing on the cabin today, but I'll make up for it, I swear. I want to talk with Mr. Winslow right away because there's not too much time, and if he likes the idea of the two churches working together, he'll want to talk with Mr. Ogilvie as soon as possible."

"Hop to it, then." Mark waved his saw. "We've done a lot today."

"Then I think I'll shove too." Sam picked up his coat. "I'll chauffeur you, Pen. I'll see you in church in the morning, Nora. So bring me my part. I have to start back right after dinner."

"I'll leave Benjie with you, Toby." Pen was slipping into her coat which Sam was holding for her. "I forgot what a popular sitter you were last summer. Mrs. Weil will be coming by here to pick him up any minute now."

CHAPTER 6

SUNDAY DAWNED CLEAR, bright and crisply cold. Nora, as usual the first one up, tiptoed across the hall to the boys' room and listened. Silence. She knocked softly, but receiving no answer, rattled the knob as she pushed the door open. Then going over to the window, she jerked it down with a bang. Mark groaned.

"I hate to cast a blight on a beautiful Sabbath morning," she caroled, "but last night we made a blood-pact. Remember? At least two hours of homework every morning before we do another thing."

"Get lost, will you, please?" Toby's voice came muffled from the bedclothes.

"All hands on deck!" Nora sounded relentless.

Mark opened one eye and sighed. "I slept and dreamed that life was beauty. I woke and found that life is duty."

Nora laughed. "I left the shower running, so it's nice and warm in the bathroom." She tweaked Toby's foot on the way out and added, "I'll make some cocoa and toast and light the fire in the living room. Be as quiet as you can when you go past Mrs. Snow's room. She likes a sleep-in Sunday mornings."

"Who doesn't!" Toby moaned, softly.

However, later, as he walked with the others down the road toward the Community church whose bells were urging them to hurry, Toby was enjoying a sense of virtue, feeling that his knowledge of American history had been vastly improved.

Even Mrs. Snow had agreed that it was too fine a morning to ride to church. Overhead little wisps of cottony white were floating in the blue sky, and the glimpses, between the houses, of the Sound were a heavenly blue too.

Nora squinted her eyes as she walked along beside Mrs. Snow and looked up at the lovely lace patterns the black and russet winter branches made against the bright sky. Undertoning the chiming of the bells she could hear the murmur of the sea against the shore and the crazy laughter of the gulls as they swooped and dove. The smooth branches of the willow trees beside the pond on the village green glowed pale lemon where the sun touched them, and Nora felt that in its own way the little town was quite as lovely in winter as it was in summer.

Sam and Pen were waiting for them in front of the church.

"I tried to get you on the phone last night," Pen said, dropping into step beside Nora.

"We went to Sundale with Mrs. Snow to help her show off the car and meet her grandchildren."

"Well, both Mr. Winslow and Mr. Ogilvie were enthusiastic about the program." Pen laughed. "Especially about keeping it short. Mr. Winslow called Mr. and Mrs. Sizer—they run Haven Academy—and they were pathetically pleased about the project because they had been afraid that Christmas was going to be a rather dismal season for them all. Then Sam had a talk with Wilson Crary—"

71

Santa Clara County Free Library
San Jose, Calif.

"He directs the Kewanaka Players," Sam explained.
"And he came up with an idea. He suggested that we use
the bandstand on the green as a stage." He nodded to it,
across the road. "He said he thought the town would get
a boot out of its being put to use again. They can rig up
some sort of sounding board at the back and sides."

"The players are going to take care of all the staging,
and the lighting too," continued Pen. "But our organist—
you know—Mrs. Fisher—wants to know what you did
about music."

"Oh." Nora stopped short. "The reason we gave it outside the church instead of outside the inn, which was traditional in old England, was so that we could use the church organ. The angel chorus was in there too. We opened some of the windows, you see."

Sam looked over at the bandstand and shook his head. "Well, that idea is out, I guess. It's too far away from the church."

"And there's no space around either of the churches." Pen bit her lip.

"I have an idea, Pen." Mrs. Snow had been listening and thinking. "Have you ever seen that little old melodeon Mrs. Fisher has in her house?"

"Yes, I have. Last summer the young people's choir often rehearsed there."

"Well," Mrs. Snow went on, "I'm pretty sure it would

fit in my station wagon if we took out two of the seats—
and Mrs. Fisher should fit too, she's so tiny—and I have a
nice little heater in the car."

"I think that might do it!" exclaimed Sam. "I'll get Wilson to put his mind to it. Did you bring my part?" he
asked Nora as they went up the church steps.

Nora pulled it out of her pocket and gave it to him. "I
hope you can read it."

"Let me see." Pen looked at the page of music Sam
had unfolded. "Ho, innkeeper, innkeeper, where are my
boys?" she was reading and singing in a low tone, but
broke off abruptly, as she heard a "Shhh." They were
walking down the aisle.

Some of the congregation twisted their heads around
to see what the disturbance was, and Mr. Winslow, who
had begun to read the opening hymn, stopped short in
surprise at the end of the first line:

"Lord of seasons, Oh! how fair—"

"He means us," Toby whispered to Mark, but changed
his mind as Mr. Winslow, looking at them over his glasses,
went on:

"Thy works; how vile thy creatures are!"

Toby shot for the first empty space he saw.

When they reached the carriage house that afternoon,
the doors were open.

"Someone must have beat us to it," said Toby, running
on ahead. Then he let out a roar. "Look what he's done
now! Just look!"

Mark and Nora burst through the doorway together.

Toby's can of green paint was tipped over on the floor, and someone had painted an ugly smear of green on the boat's white hull.

"We could have him arrested for that!"

"Who?" Nora picked up Dinghy, who was about to investigate the green pool.

"Joel!" Toby roared. "Who else would play a dirty trick like that? I told you he could get dangerous."

"Rubbish!" Nora's voice was sharp. "Maybe a dog wandered in and tipped the can over."

"How many dogs do you know who can handle a paint brush?" Mark was dabbing at the smeared hull with a rag soaked in turpentine.

"Holy cow!" Spike was standing in the doorway staring. "What happened?"

"Joel—he—he—" Toby was so enraged he could only splutter.

"Somebody must have accidentally knocked the can over," Nora told him.

"Accidentally, my eye!" Toby's voice had come back. "I know how to put paint away. I jumped on the cover and turned it over to seal it. And that smear was painted on. Look—" He picked up a paint brush that was lying on the edge of the puddle. "He used this." He looked up as a shadow fell through the doorway.

Joel was standing there, his mouth open, a newspaper bundle under his arm.

"You big jerk!" Toby started for him, waving the paint brush menacingly. "It would serve you right if I went down and smeared up your boat."

Joel closed his mouth and put up one hand as Toby advanced. Toby stopped short and stared at it. Then he turned to Nora. "Now will you believe he did it? Look at that paint on him. We've caught him red-handed!"

"Green-handed, you mean." Spike giggled.

"If you ever come in here again—"

"Who owns this place, anyway?" Joel's voice was soft as he sneered down at Toby, but his face was flushing. He started to say something else, but after looking at the accusing eyes of the others, turned on his heel and walked away.

"I'm going over and tell Mr. Thurston—" Toby began, but Mark shook his head.

"Skip it," he said. "Get busy with some rags before the stuff dries on us."

"Do you mean you're letting him get away with this?" Toby squeaked.

"If he did it, he knows we know and won't try anything like that again."

"If!" Toby was still squeaking. "It figures, doesn't it?"

"You can't condemn a man on circumstantial evidence alone. Spike, you'd better get some kindling and coal and start the fire. Norie, would you bring over a bunch of those newspapers?" Mark nodded toward a pile of them. "No use ruining all these clean rags."

"We ought to put a padlock on the doors," Toby muttered.

"Oh, fiddle-dee-dee!" Nora put Dinghy down on the swing. "Nobody in Kewanaka ever locks their doors."

Mark was taking a breather, lying in the bottom of the sloop flat on his back and half listening to Nora teaching the "three little boys" their song to the accompaniment of sandpaper rubbing on wood.

"Oh, please, Mr. Innkeeper, please let us in, for the night is so dark and so cold—"

But Mark's mind was really on the cabin. As he looked up at the sturdy oak framework arching over him, he was thinking that the cabin was going to be quite as fine as he had planned it.

They had all been working hard all afternoon, and when Mr. Thurston had put his head in the door to see what progress had been made, he had told them that at the rate they were going he would not be surprised if the cabin were finished long before Christmas.

Now Star, on her way back from the lumber pile with a length of oak trim, was looking down at Mark. "Port and I used to do that sometimes." She laughed. "Pretending we were sleeping in a cabin." She ran her hand over the frames and shook them. "At last I really believe we're going to have one. Until you put the framing up, it just seemed like a dream. What are you going to do next?"

"Get the pipes for the berths and make the supports for them. So you and Nora had better get busy stitching the canvas."

"It was good of you and Mrs. Snow to give us your canvas."

"A mere bagatelle." Mark stood up, then winced. He put his tongue between his teeth and let out a shrill whistle. "Time to knock off, crew!"

"We'll have to paint her all over again, I guess." Star was looking at the smeared place on the hull that Mark had only succeeded in making paler.

He nodded. "It just needs one coat. That won't be any chore at all. We'll do that when we paint the sides of the cabin."

"When everything's finished, do you suppose we could put her over and try her out?"

Mark grinned. "Why? Do you want to make sure she won't buck you overboard?"

Star reddened a little. "That Joel! Sometimes when he says things like that, he sounds so convincing. Ouch!"

"Oh, golly, I'm sorry." Toby had been collecting the finished lengths of oak round and had poked Star in the ribs with them.

"Here, let me help you." Star drew some from under his arm. "Let's put them over there away from the un-done ones."

Toby looked at the pile of "un-done" ones and groaned. "My, gosh, there are yards and yards still to do. Give me that one you were going to start, and I'll put it back. Say, listen, Star, I've been wondering— What are your real names?"

Star looked at him out of the corners of her eyes. "I'll tell you when you tell me why you're called Toby."

Toby looked at her suspiciously. "I bet someone's already told you." He looked over at Ted. "Ted did!"

"No, he didn't." Star shook her head. "I asked him, and he said he didn't know, but from the way he said it, I was sure he did."

Toby looked at Ted again. "Nice character!" Then he grinned at Star. "Guess."

Star laughed. "Twenty Questions?"

Toby nodded. "Though you'll never guess unless you know your Sha— Well, start guessing. It's not vegetable or mineral."

"Then it's animal." Star rubbed her chin. "Were you named after someone?"

Toby nodded. "Yes."

"A member of the family—or some family friend?"

Toby shook his head. "No."

Star thought a moment. "Were you named after anyone at all or—or some *thing?*"

"That's two questions."

"Okay. Were you named after something like—like a Toby jug, for instance— I mean did your ears stick out and—"

"No! I've always had lovely ears!" Toby felt them. "Besides a jug isn't animal."

"That's right. But you did get the nickname when you were a baby?"

Toby nodded.

Star thought again, and then said, "Were you named for a fictional character?"

"You're getting warmer."

Star opened her mouth, closed it, and opening it again, stabbed a finger at him. "Sir Toby Belch! I know I'm right. You eat so much!"

"That's an unkind remark." Toby looked grieved.

"But I guessed it, didn't I?"

Toby nodded, reluctantly.

"I'm sorry, Toby. I didn't mean it—about your eating so much. Just for that I'll *tell* you our names, if you promise not to give it away."

"I promise."

"Well, Port's name is Cassandra, and mine's Cressida. They're out of Shakespeare too. That's why I guessed so soon. Imagine! Cressy and Cassy! Wouldn't that be something? Almost as corny as if we dressed alike."

"Beep—beep!"

Toby rushed to a window and, cupping his hands over his eyes, peered out. "It's Mrs. Snow and her jalopy," he announced.

"Don't call it that," Nora scolded. "You might forget and say it in front of her."

And then Mrs. Snow was there. "My, you *are* coming along!" She went over to the boat and examined it closely. "It's a real shipbuilding job. Well, I see you're about ready to leave." She had turned to Ted who was putting on his leather jacket. "Your mother told me to tell you they're having supper at the Cavanaughs'. So, if you'll take pot luck with us—"

"You bet." Ted grinned. "Thanks a lot."

"Come along, Harvey," she said to the first little boy. "I told Mrs. Sizer I'd see that you got back. Can we drop anyone else?"

"Spike and I came on our bikes," Flossie told her.

"Why not toss them in the jalopy," said Mrs. Snow. "What do you suppose I got a station wagon for?"

"Okay." Spike grinned at Nora. "It's a hard pump up to my house."

CHAPTER 7

A WEEK HAD ROLLED around since they had started on the cabin. So far nobody's interest had flagged, and each afternoon, after school, the three little boys had worked and sung with the innkeeper and his wife, with Mark also giving the Saint Nicholas cues. Sometimes Pen and Star and Ted were late, as they were also having their rehearsals at the church. Ted was King Melchior, and Star was one of the three angels who were going to be on the stage. Several of the older boys and girls from the academy had come in afternoons to help too—they attended the schools in town. Only the lower grades were taught at the academy. All the sheathing was now on. Just yesterday they had put a gross and a half of screws in the cabin top.

This Saturday afternoon Nora and Star were rummaging through the lumber pile for pieces of pine to make the long narrow shelves above the berths when Mrs. Snow came in.

"Conor O'Brien has invited anyone who can and wants to, to have tea with him this afternoon," she announced. "And you're to come just as you are, he says."

"Is there a Mrs. O'Brien?" Toby asked her.

"No. There hasn't been for more years than I like to remember." She turned to Nora. "If you people want to go, I think I'll drive over to my daughter's and sit for them so they can get out for a few hours."

"Don't hurry back," Nora said. "I can get supper."

Pen laughed. "It's easy to see you've never had tea at Mr. O'Brien's. He calls it 'high tea,' which is almost equivalent to a banquet. You won't need any supper tonight."

"Oh, boy! Where does he live?" Toby asked.

"Do you know that little house perched on the side of the bluff where the creek goes into the bay?" asked Mrs. Snow.

"That darling little weather-shingled cottage you have to climb down to from the road?" exclaimed Nora.

Mrs. Snow nodded. "That's it."

"What time does he want us?" Toby was looking at his watch. "I'm feeling kind of peckish."

"When aren't you?" Mark growled from inside the cabin.

"He said any time." Mrs. Snow was looking at her watch too. "Do you think you could knock off early for once, Mark?" She put her head through one of the holes that had been cut for the port lights. "I'd like to get started for Sundale as soon as possible."

Mark was lying on his back trying out one of the berths that he had lashed to the pipes. "You don't have to drive us, Mrs. Snow. Why don't you get going?"

"But it's so far—"

"There's no use our holding you up, Mrs. Snow," said Pen. "We'll find someone to drive us. Though it wouldn't hurt us to walk."

"Very well, then. But I'll have to take you along with me, Harvey. Mrs. Sizer will be expecting you."

"My mother's picking Flossie and me up. We have to

get dressed for dancing school." Spike made a rude noise to show his opinion of that. "We'll see that Harvey gets home."

"Fine. Someone had better call Conor as soon as possible to tell him how many to expect."

"I'll phone from our house, Mrs. Snow," Star assured her.

"I declare I can never get over how much you do each day." Mrs. Snow was looking around as she pulled on her gloves.

Mark was a good general, and all the helpers were busy at the jobs that suited them best.

Nora stopped sawing and pushed the hair back from her forehead. "Many hands make light work, you know." She gave a little half laugh. "To coin a cliché."

"There's the Mad Hatter again!" exclaimed Toby. "Gee, he looks cold. Doesn't he own a winter coat?"

"Who?"

"That's what Nora calls the character with the ears," Toby explained to Mrs. Snow. "The one who used to collect rents for Mr. Fleet."

Mrs. Snow laughed and went out. "Hello, Ferd Snively," they heard her say. "They told me at the garage that you'd left town. Can I give you a lift somewhere?" Then Ted, who had opened the doors for her, banged them together.

The work was going so much faster than anyone had anticipated that Mark did call a halt early that day, and there was still some cold gray daylight left when the Brices with Pen and Ted arrived on foot at Mr. O'Brien's little cottage. Toby had been carrying Dinghy the last

83

quarter of a mile because he was sure the long walk had tired him.

Star had offered to telephone Ted's house and Pen's to tell them not to wait supper, but she could not join the tea party as she had to stay and get her father's supper.

As Nora climbed down the seven steps from the road, she thought that the front of the little house, perched so precariously up over the water, looked like a jolly face and said so.

The others stopped for a moment and looked to see what she meant.

"I get it." Toby squinted his eyes. "The steps are his chins, but the top one's his grin. The door is his fat nose."

"The little windows on either side with the light behind them are twinkling eyes," said Pen.

"And the roof is his cocked hat," Mark contributed. "The kind kids make out of newspaper."

Just then Mr. O'Brien, looking like a great cinnamon bear in his comfortable brown tweed jacket, came around the side of the house, and although he did not know what they were laughing at, he laughed with them anyway, because he loved entertaining company—especially young company. Which may have been because he had never had any young ones of his own.

"It's grand t' have ye aboard," he told them. "I've been givin' me wee birdies their tea. Come out back an' see 'em before ye go in. Quiet now! *Cave canem*," he whispered to Dinghy, who was still tucked under Toby's arm, and chuckled softly as he led the way around.

Back there, dark trees, twisted into fantastic shapes by the storms that frequently whipped up high seas and torrential rains over the Sound in the fall of the year, stood like giant gnomes, misshapen, but friendly. Friendly, because their crooked arms were bent over the little cottage as though protecting it from the wild elements. Under the trees and between them were bird houses and feeding stations.

"Look now, would ye! Just look at that little thief!" Conor O'Brien exclaimed under his breath, nodding toward a gray squirrel who was inching out on a limb, obviously trying to get at a lump of suet on a tray suspended from it.

However, two birds, perched on the edge of the tray, caught sight of him and burst into such a shrill cacophony of scolding that he turned his bushy tail and scurried away, his plume waving like a flag.

"Serves you right, greedy little pig. I put out nuts fer the likes of you." Mr. O'Brien chuckled. "Them starlin's is the noisiest birds known t' man—always jabberin'. I once had one could say Conor plain as I can."

"You mean they can talk like parrots?" Toby exclaimed.

Mr. O'Brien nodded. "Some can."

"And I'll have me a starling who's one word will be—" Nora stopped. "There's something like that—in Shakespeare, I think—but I've forgotten it."

"What are those little birds coming down the tree trunks upside down?" asked Toby.

"My upside down birds. They're as friendly as can be." Mr. O'Brien made a soft trilling noise. "They're nuthatches."

"I'm almost positive I saw a scarlet tanager yesterday," Nora told him. "Imagine in December. I couldn't believe my eyes."

Mr. O'Brien nodded his head. "Either some of the birds

85

stay with us longer and longer each year, or they come back t' us sooner. I don't rightly know which."

"Listen to the downies." Pen held up her hand. "They're pecking at the trees looking for their tea."

Then they all heard.

"Tap—tap—tap-tap-tap—"

"Look at my little chickadees, over there in their little black bibs an' caps, gobblin' the sunflower seeds. Fer all they're so tiny, they go fer them seeds like they was ostriches." Mr. O'Brien began to chirp. "Chick-a-dee, chick-a-dee-dee-dee."

One of the little birds stopped gobbling long enough to answer him. "Chick-a-dee—chick-a-dee-dee-dee-dee-dee." Then it went back to gobbling all the faster.

"Just lookin' at 'em makes me want my tea." Mr. O'Brien laughed and waved them into the house through the kitchen door.

"Hi!" Nora called out as she went in. "We haven't seen you in ages."

Toby, who was following on her heels, stopped short and glowered. Joel was standing alongside the kitchen table.

"Don't blow a gasket." Mark prodded Toby from behind.

"Would those of ye who have not been here before want t' be lookin' around at me few treasures before ye have yer tay?" Mr. O'Brien's brogue thickened as he played the host. "Or is iveryone starvin'?"

"Toby probably is," Nora said. "But that's not news. Let's look around first."

Dinghy made a beeline for the warm hearth in the

living room and curled up in a ball, as soon as Toby put him down.

After they had hung their coats on the rack in the tiny hall, they followed Mr. O'Brien back to the living room, and Nora and Toby peeked into the small bedroom that opened out of it. Besides the kitchen—and the bathroom, of course—that was the whole house.

Now Nora was admiring a collection of oddly colored bottles on the mantel that glittered in the lamp light.

"Me youngest brother—the one who migrated t' the west as soon as we come over from the old sod—brought me them." Mr. O'Brien was looking at the bottles too. "He says they got them colors from layin' around in the desert sands. Pretty, ain't they?"

"Gosh, do you smoke all those?" Toby was gazing at one of the walls beside the fireplace on which dozens of clay pipes of all lengths and shapes hung in racks.

Mr. O'Brien chuckled. "I don't smoke at all. 'Tis a collection I started as a lad, an' people keep bringin' 'em t' me. Them there with the crazy faces is gargoyles. They're from France, an' them at that end is Eyetalian."

"Did you make the racks yourself?" Toby went over to examine them closely.

"I did."

"I made a little one for Father for Christmas." Toby shook his head. "But it's not as fine as these."

Nora knelt on the floor and put her ear to a huge conch shell lying in the corner of the hearth. "It sounds just like the sea breaking on the shore."

"You Brices must be honored guests." Pen was looking at the Turkey red cloth that covered the big round table in front of the fire. It was embroidered with intricate

patterns of green, gold and silver threads. "Mr. O'Brien doesn't display that very often. It's his travel cloth."

Three pair of eyes looked their question at him.

"We had it at home in Ireland," Mr. O'Brien explained. "It's so old the gold an' silver is tarnished, but I remember when they was bright. Ye see, the O'Brien boys was always hankerin' t' travel an' see the world, so our Da' invented a game. Each week one of us would choose a place we'd like t' see, an' we'd study about it in our books. Then, on Sunday nights, our Mam would get out the cloth fer a special treat. She set great store by it because a sea captain had brought it to her from some far place, an' she'd only break it out on Sundays an' such. Then we'd have a fine old time sittin' around it an' goin' places. That's why we called it the travel cloth. Y'see," he went on, "there was no TV or radio—not even movies when I was a lad. Oh, I've seen many wonderful changes in me long life, but I still like t' play the old game by meself now and then."

"Have you traveled a lot?" Mark asked him.

"What d'ye think I do most of the days of the week? That's travelin', ain't it?" Mr. O'Brien's eyes twinkled. "Well, now that y've seen all there is t' see, how about tay? One of the wonderful changes I've seen in respect t' that is these here instant things. So I can offer ye a choice of beverages all outa the same kettle. Ye can have tay-tay like what I'm havin' fer instance, an' it won't be none of that stuff that comes in nasty little bags. It'll be the real thing. Or ye can have coffee-tay, an' I can offer ye chocolarity-tay too."

"If you have any marshmallows, I'll have chocolarity-tay," said Toby.

Nora frowned at him, but Mr. O'Brien nodded.

"I have some. Tell ye what—" He picked up a white cloth, lying over the back of a chair and spread it over the travel cloth. "I'll bring in all the things an' ye can help y'selves. The kettle should soon be on the bile."

"Can we help you?" Nora asked.

Mr. O'Brien paused on his way to the kitchen. "In a man's house, the galley's no place fer a woman."

"I'll help you then." Toby followed him out. "Did you remember to look and see if you had any old charts lying around, Mr. O'Brien?"

"I found some of a cruise I'd made once t' Canada."

"Canada!"

"Well, let's say New Brunswick. It's the bit of Canada that's nearest Maine, but it's Canada, all right."

To Toby, charts of any cruises outside of Long Island Sound were important enough to collect.

"I hope ye all like an egg t' yer tay, same as I do, because I'm makin' the spesh-ee-ality of the house—Spanish omelet." Mr. O'Brien took down the largest skillet Toby had ever seen from a nail on the wall.

While Mr. O'Brien got things out of the icebox, Toby wandered over to the window sill where a row of little white oblong cakes covered with seeds were lined up. "Gosh, these look good." He reached for one.

"They are." Joel had come into the kitchen. "Try one— that's what they're there for."

Toby picked one up and was about to bite into it, then glanced at Joel, suspiciously.

Mr. O'Brien took his head out of the icebox and chuckled. "I see ye've found me little upside down birds' favorite cakes. I make 'em meself of suet an' birdseed.

Oh, how the little spalpeens love 'em. The fat keeps 'em warm in winter."

Toby put the cake carefully back on the window sill, and without looking at Joel, went over to the table to help with the omelet.

During tea, egged on by Pen and Ted, Mr. O'Brien told them stories of his boyhood days on the west coast of Ireland, and stories he had been told by his father to whom many of them had been told by his father before him—strange tales of the wee people who flitted about the bogs at night. And while he washed the tea things and the boys dried them, the girls stood in the doorway listening to him boom one Irish sea chanty after another.

After the last cup had been hung on its hook, they all trooped back to the living room, and though Mr. O'Brien was protesting that his throat was hoarse from all his talking and singing, Pen begged for one last song.

"Pharaoh's Daughter," she begged. "Please, Mr. O'Brien."

"Well, then, if ye'll just give me time t' push the table forninst the wall over there, I'll oblige ye. But it'll be the last ye'll be gettin' out of me this day."

"We'll take care of the table." Ted took hold of one side and Mark the other, and as they went over to sprawl on the hearth rug beside Nora and Pen, Mr. O'Brien leaned back in his big, red leather chair and began to sing.

"Whin Pharaoh's daughter wint down t' the wather,
Sure there was young Moses a-shwimmin' around
In his arruk so handy, wid a shtick of swate candy,
T' kape him from cryin' ontil he was found.

Says she to a maithen, says she, 'Bring yon haythen,
    Yer trotters be shakin', ye lazy spalpeen;
If the wathers wance wet him, or the crocodiles get him,
    It's no crocodile tears ye'll be sheddin', I ween.'

So, whin from his shwimmin' he was brought t' the
        wimmin'
    Faith, it shows how the blarney's a famale's chafe joy,
A nate bow he was makin', as sure as I'm spakin;
    'Begorra!' says she, 'he's the broth of a boy.'"

"Now then," he said, after the applause and laughter had subsided. "Let's hear about *your* doin's fer a change."

So they took turns telling him about the cabin and the Christmas program—all that is except Joel, who was sitting on a straight chair in the shadow of the chimney saying nothing, and watching Toby, several charts spread out on the floor, crawling over them like Pelorus Jack leading ships into harbor. However, all of them, even Toby, carefully refrained from telling about the spilled paint episode.

Mr. O'Brien nodded when they seemed to have run down. "I heard about the pageant an' the little opera from Sam when he come in fer a minute Satiddy night. So I've been drummin' up some extra int'rest in the academy all along the line. Of course few if any of them folks that don't live around here will be comin' t' the program, Christmas Eve, but I figgered maybe some of 'em might think t' send checks." His eyes twinkled shrewdly. Then, as if he realized that Joel had been left out, he turned to him and said, "Are you takin' part in the program, lad?"

Joel's lips tightened as he got to his feet. "No. Did you ever see a character in a Christmas pageant wearing glasses?" His voice was like sandpaper on varnished wood. "I have to go. Thanks for asking me, Mr. O'Brien. I'll let myself out."

Deep silence filled the little house until the front door slammed; then there was a general clearing of throats.

"Did he know we were going to be here when you invited him, Mr. O'Brien?" Toby finally said.

"No. I was hopin' that, over tea, ye could maybe get t' be friends like."

"We offered him the part of one of the kings," Pen said. "He has a good voice and he doesn't have to wear those glasses. In fact, Dr. Adams says they're bad for his eyes."

"I still don't understand why he acts as he does," said Nora. "He seems to go out of his way to feel sorry for himself, and at the same time make other people dislike him. He was fun to crew for—"

"Fun! When he almost—"

"Shut up, Tobe." Mark reached out and nudged him with his toe.

"I still think he's dangerous," Toby muttered to himself as he folded up his charts.

Mr. O'Brien sighed. "Poor Joel. He's just what he am an' nothin' but an eye surgeon, maybe, could make him a bit am-er. He's always wanted t' go t' Annapolis, but ye got t' have good eyes t' get in the Navy."

There had been another uncomfortable little silence until, with a loud pop, the big back log broke into a mass of glowing coals that came flying out on to the wide hearth, startling the people lying around it.

"The fire's perfect fer poppin' corn now, if anyone's int'rested." Mr. O'Brien was brushing the coals off the rug.

Ted looked at his watch. "My gosh, it's almost seven! We ought to be going. Anyway, I'm so full, I couldn't even eat popcorn. We'll walk you home first, Pen, since you live nearest, and I'm practically next door to the Fo'c's'le."

"This was a wonderful break in the day's occupation, Mr. O'Brien." Nora got stiffly to her feet. "I'm glad there's a short-cut home."

"You sure bake an elegant cake," Toby told him.

"Me car's gettin' a goin' over at the garage or I'd run ye all home." Mr. O'Brien followed them out the door and squinted at the sky. "Fer all the moon's bright, it feels like we might be gettin' some snow," he commented.

"Yippee!" Toby had handed Mark his charts and was lifting Dinghy to carry him up the steep steps. "Maybe I'll get in some skiing then."

"Thank you—thank you again—thanks a million, Mr. O'Brien—it was terrific—" they called back to him from the road. And after Toby had put him down, Dinghy expressed his thanks too, in staccato barks, for the tidbits that had been handed him.

After they had left Pen at her house, the others climbed until they were on the bluff that topped the bay. Ted's house was the next stop because the Fo'c's'le was farther along.

They stood for a moment saying their good-nights and looking up at the icy gray sky and the broad path of dazzling silver that led out to where the moon hung clear and bright over the changing water of the bay. Toby was hopefully looking for clouds full of snow.

CHAPTER 8

OBY DID NOT HAVE to be awakened the next morning. Mr. O'Brien's prediction as to the weather had proved right. Long before they had gone to bed, snow began to fall. And though the snowflakes melted as soon as they fell to the ground, Toby was so confident that he would wake up to a white world that he spent an hour waxing his skis in front of the fireplace. At first when he opened his eyes, he thought they must have overslept. The room was brilliant with light. Then he remembered and glanced at the window, where white snow lay deep along the sill. Throwing back the covers, he rushed over to look out. Everything on land was somehow hushed, as though muffled by the billowing sea of white spread over it. Even the gulls seemed to be holding their breath this morning. The lower branches of the two big fir trees were pressed to the ground by the weight of the snow they carried. He shut the window, which they had only opened a crack the night before, and scarcely noticed the cold snow that he had dislodged melting on his bare feet. Grabbing Mark's shoulder, he shook him awake.

"Wha—? Wha—?" Mark woke up yelling.

"Look!" Toby's teeth were chattering more from excitement than cold. He had been missing the Wisconsin winter of snow and ice. "It's been snowing all night and it hasn't stopped yet. How about a polar expedition, Marco Polo?"

Mark blinked at the whiteness and grinned. "I can see that we're not going to get much work out of you today."

"Spike said Charley promised to take over for me, because I was going to finish Mrs. Snow's Christmas present today." Toby dug into his duffel bag and pulled out a large wooden spoon and fork. "The spoon's done, but gosh, I wish I'd done the fork first. I'm sick of sandpapering and it'll take me forever to get the tines smooth."

"It's time Charley showed up. I'll work the jeans off him. Let me see the fork." Mark took it from him and rubbed the smooth handle, appreciatively, between his fingers. "Um—a nice hunk of seasoned apple. I tell you what, Tobe. I'll put in a little time on it for you today."

"You will? Gee, swell! I promised to give Flossie a skiing lesson the first day it snowed." Toby was already pulling his ski pants out of the duffel bag.

"The snow will probably be too soft for good skiing." Mark laughed. "But Flossie won't mind that when she falls down."

On his way downstairs, Toby thumped on Nora's door. "Are you decent?" he bawled, and without waiting for an answer, pushed the door open. But Nora was not there. Then he heard her talking in the hall below and looked over the railing. Nora, in her bathrobe, was just hanging up the telephone.

"It was Father," she said, when she caught sight of him. "I thought he was phoning to say he'd be out to see us today, but he's flying to San Francisco. I hardly got a chance to say much more than hello. Publishers! Honestly!"

"When's he coming back?"

"He said he'd surely be here Christmas Eve."

Toby nodded as he started down the stairs. "He'd better be. Look, Nora, I'm going to pick up Flossie and Spike. We're going skiing on Johnny Cake Hill, so I'll just grab me a glass of milk and some bread and peanut butter and slither along."

"You'll slither out of that pea jacket and into the kitchen first." Mrs. Snow was standing at the end of the hall. "You're not going out into that until you have something warm under your belt." She was looking out the hall windows where flurries of snow were being blown by the wind.

"The amount he consumes, he should be able to live on his own fat for a while—the way bears do." Nora went upstairs to get dressed.

"Don't worry about Flossie and Spike," she heard Mrs. Snow say. "Why do you suppose I'm up so early of a Sunday? They telephoned just before your father did. I told them you'd be along soon enough."

"You're in rare luck," Mrs. Snow went on to Toby after they were in the kitchen. "It isn't often we have snow so early. It usually comes just when we're longing for the sight of snowdrops and crocuses pushing up through the earth."

Nora and Mark came down to have a "civilized" breakfast—as Mrs. Snow called it—just as Toby was leaving with his skis over his shoulder and his navy blue watch cap tilted rakishly over one eye.

"That cap's not going to keep your ears from freezing if you don't pull it down," Mrs. Snow warned him.

"Oh, no, Mrs. Snow!" Mark was grinning. "That wouldn't look nautical."

"And it would hide his lovely ears," said Nora.

Toby paused on his way out the door and looked at her. "You were listening to Star and me when we played Twenty Questions," he accused.

"It's all right. Star told me their real names ages ago. Have fun, Toby."

"You'll have to put up with us today, Dink." Mark scooped up the eager little dog to keep him from following Toby. "You're not a Saint Bernard, fella."

Mark had shoveled a path down the porch steps and the walk, and he had cleared the driveway too, for the snow plow had been through the roads, and Mrs. Snow was driving them to church.

Toby did not show up until just as they were sitting down to dinner. "I don't have to wash," he announced, sliding into his place at the table and looking at his reddened hands. "I've been making snowballs. It's good packing."

"How was the skiing?" Mrs. Snow handed him his soup.

"The slope would be okay if it were only much longer. You just begin to get going when you have to stop." Toby tipped a spoonful of the hot liquid into his mouth and let it trickle warmly down his throat before he went on. "But we had fun anyway. Gee, Ralph Bergman and Al Monroe—he's Harvey's brother, the one who's going to be the Ethiopian king—fixed up an old beat-up gasoline engine they found somewhere and rigged a ski tow. It's neat. Ralph sure is a brain. He's getting a scholarship for college, but he can't make up his mind whether to go in for engineering or be a philosopher."

"Do you have to slurp your soup?" Nora was shaking her head at him. "Why can't Ralph be both?"

"Who is this Ralph?" Mrs. Snow reached over and replaced Toby's soup plate with another.

"He and his sister, Miriam, live at the academy," Nora explained. "Pen brought them in one afternoon to work on the cabin, but they have jobs after school at the academy, so we've never seen them since. They're going to be Joseph and Mary in the pageant, and they're perfect for the parts. They look like biblical characters—especially Ralph."

Mrs. Snow shook her head. "I haven't had a chance to get acquainted with many of those young folks, but Ralph sounds like the boy Mr. Weil is so interested in."

"He's the one. Mr. Weil got him his scholarship for the college he went to." Toby swallowed the lump of roast beef he had been chewing while he talked.

"Honestly, Toby! You remind me of Mr. O'Brien's chickadees. You're bolting your food like an ostrich!" Nora was making clucking sounds against the roof of her mouth.

"Well, you sound like an old mother hen," Toby retorted through a mouthful of mashed potatoes. "I have to get back to the slope. Harvey thinks he can dig up a pair of boots so he can borrow my skis."

"I wonder where Benjie Weil has been." Nora was trying not to watch Toby load his fork with peas, with the help of a surreptitious thumb. "I thought he'd be coming in all the time to help us paint. He lives near enough the carriage house to get himself there."

"Maybe his mother thinks he might make a nuisance of himself," suggested Mrs. Snow.

Nora nodded. "Maybe."

"I'll stop at his house and invite him specially." Toby lifted his fork to his mouth without losing a single pea.

"How did Flossie do?" Mark asked after Toby had passed his plate up for seconds.

"At the rate she's going, she'll be on the nursery slope the rest of her life. She's a real snow bunny. All she does is fall down and giggle."

"What do you think you did when you were learning?"

"When *I* was learning?" Toby looked at Nora in surprise. "Gee, I can't ever remember not being able to ski."

"Well, Mark and I can, and you not only fell down most of the time and giggled, but you also fell down and lost your temper and howled. So don't be so superior." Nora was glad of the chance to get back at Toby for his questionable table manners.

Mark knew it and grinned to himself. "Does Spike do all right?" he asked him.

"Fairly good." Toby glanced over at Nora as he took his plate from Mrs. Snow. "In fact he's very good," he added, hastily. "He's got so he can start from the top, anyway. Golly, if it weren't for the road, it would be a pretty good slope. You could go all the way down to the cove over the steepest part of the golf course."

"Who else was skiing?" Nora asked him.

"Just Ted and some girl who's in his class at school. They're really keen."

"Oh, foo! Now I wish we'd brought our skis, Mark."

"I thought you'd feel that way." Toby's round eyes blinked at Nora over the rim of his glass as he noisily gulped his milk. Now he had got back at her!

✦

Although Mark and Nora would have preferred to walk back through the drifts from the carriage house that evening, Mrs. Snow had called for them in the car.

Now Nora was on her way upstairs to clean up for supper. As she passed the boys' room, she paused. Toby was in there, his back to her. He was draped in Mark's topcoat and looking at himself in the mirror over the dresser.

"What in the world!" she exclaimed.

Toby turned around. "The Small Fry Club is having a dance at the yacht club Christmas week—before that dance you and Mark are going to with Ted and Star—and I've been invited."

"Is it a masquerade?"

"No, of course it isn't." Toby shook himself out of the coat and hung it back in the closet. "Only I can't wear a pea jacket to a dance, can I?"

"At least it fits you," said Nora. "I told you to bring your gabardine."

"Well, golly! How could I know that Spike and Flossie would be going social? They didn't go in for that stuff at all last summer." Toby sat down on his bed.

"Don't worry. I'll drop Father a note to bring your coat when he comes."

"Do you think my gray flannel suit will be all right for an evening party? It's from seven to nine. Spike's wearing navy blue."

"Gray flannel is very smart for evening wear this season." Nora's lips twitched a little. "Are you taking Flossie?"

"Flossie! Yikes, no! I might as well be taking Spike. She asked me though."

"Then who are you taking? I mean *whom*."

"Flossie asked Spike to take a cousin of hers who's going to be visiting them that week—that's why her mother's making Flossie go to the dance. But Spike wouldn't bite. He said he had a blind date once before, and she turned out to be an awful hag."

"So you're being noble and taking Flossie's cousin off his hands?" Nora looked puzzled.

Toby looked up from the boot he was unlacing and smirked. "I saw the gal's picture, and Spike didn't, so he's stuck with Flossie. Say, Nora, how do you get started on a blind date? I mean, what do you talk about?"

"You could quote some poetry. Girls usually like that." Nora leaned against the door jamb, her forehead corrugated in thought. "Let me see—I have it! Just suppose when you and Spike go to call for them, the girls are still upstairs primping. As they're coming down the stairs, Flossie introduces you to her cousin. Then you look up and catch your breath." Nora caught hers dramatically. "Then you could toss off something like this—

> *"Haste thee, Nymph, and bring with thee*
> *Jest and youthful Jollity*
> *Quips and Cranks and wanton wiles*
> *Nods and Beaks and wreathed Smiles."*

"Haste thee, nymph!" Toby threw back his head and rolled his eyes heavenward. "Oh, Nooooo!"

"I thought only certain four-legged animals bayed at the moon." Mark, who had followed Nora upstairs, had been listening. "I have something for you, Tobe, that will really send her. It's appropriate too. Girls always douse themselves with perfume for a dance." Mark struck a pose in the doorway.

> *"I counted two and seventy stenches*
> *All well defined and several stinks—"*

"Watch out, Mark!" Nora ducked as Toby's heavy boot came sailing toward them.

Mark caught it and laughed. "I don't think you'll have any trouble thinking up subjects to talk about, fella. Only thing to remember is—give the girl a chance to put in a word now and then. Here, catch!" He dropped the boot and tossed the wooden fork in Toby's direction.

"Oh, my gosh!" Toby picked it up as it fell on the bed beside him. "You finished it. It's terrific, Mark."

"You can make up for the hours I sweated over it by painting the inside of the cabin tomorrow."

"Is it all finished inside?" Toby looked up.

Nora nodded. "The cupboards and the book shelf—everything's done in there. It's going to look grand when it's painted white. Mark's making the hatch cover now and Ted's putting in the binnacle."

"Then what's to do?"

"White lead," Mark answered Toby. "And white lead—and more white lead—pounds of it to make the cabin watertight."

Toby shuddered. "Remind me the next time there's a cabin to be built to drop dead or something first. Well, I'd better wash up." He started for the bathroom in his stocking feet, then stopped. "Holy grommet! I almost forgot. The kids at the academy are throwing a wing-ding tomorrow night. They're going to sweep off the lake—or

Santa Clara County Free Library
San Jose, Calif.

part of it anyway—for skating, and have a dog roast. Anybody can come, only we'll have to take our own mess."

"Wonderful! I'm glad we brought our skates anyway." Nora glanced at the window. "There'll be a full moon."

"Look, Nora." Toby cleared his throat and looked sidelong at her. "After supper will you help me brush up on my dancing?"

"We're rehearsing the Saint Nicholas play at Mrs. Fisher's tonight, and I have to teach her that song Benjie's going to sing so she can write it down. But if we get back early enough, I'll be glad to."

The next day on his way to work, Toby remembered his favorite "sittee" again. He was feeling rather smug as he rang the Weils' doorbell, because he had finished all his school assignments that morning.

Mrs. Weil came to the door. "Hello there, Toby. Come in."

"I can't stay, Mrs. Weil, and I don't want to track snow into the house. No, Dink!" Toby thrust out a snowy ski boot to prevent Dinghy from going inside. "I just stopped by to tell Benjie to hop into his oldest jeans and come over to the carriage house if he'd like to help me paint."

"That's kind of you, Toby. He told me you'd invited him to help and to learn a song for the program." Mrs. Weil looked troubled. "But he isn't feeling very well. He won't go to kindergarten and when he saw you coming up the walk, he started to cry and ran upstairs."

"Oh, gosh, I'm sorry, Mrs. Weil. What does the doctor say?"

"I'm taking him to Dr. Adams this afternoon." Mrs. Weil looked puzzled. "For some reason, he doesn't seem

104

to mind going there, though he usually hates being examined."

"Well, golly, I hope it's nothing much. Tell him to come around just as soon as he's feeling better. Good-bye, Mrs. Weil." Toby waved, and tucking Dinghy under his arm, started away through the deepest drifts he could find.

The Brices and Star and Ted were the last to leave the carriage house that day. The others had gone home to collect their skates and their suppers before going to the lake. But Mrs. Snow was packing supper for all of them because she and Mr. Thurston were having theirs at the Chases'.

"There'll be hardly anything for Sam to do when he gets here this week." Toby was examining the runners for the hatch cover that Mark had screwed to either side of the companionway.

"There's still plenty to do," said Mark. "He can cement the canvas on the cabin top, and there's the trim to put on and varnish."

"And the outside to paint," Ted put in. "And there's always white leading. You can never put in too much of that stuff."

"Beep—beep."

Toby looked up. "That must be Mrs. Snow and her dog sled. I hope she remembered to bring my skis along. Spike and Flossie and I are going to spend our time on the slope."

"Come on!" Nora was standing impatiently by the door alongside of Star who was carrying her skates over her shoulder.

"Okay—okay."

Mrs. Snow had remembered Toby's skis and Mark's and Nora's skates. She had also packed their three knapsacks with frankfurters and buttered rolls and cake, and had taken both the big thermos jugs they used in *Scud* and filled them with hot cocoa.

So in less than no time, they were at the foot of the ski slope, looking very much like a "polar expedition" with their jeans tucked into their boots, and Mark, Nora and Ted carrying the knapsacks strapped to their backs. Mark and Ted were toting the heavy jugs, and Star was carrying their skates.

Flossie waved to them from the bump that topped what was obviously the nursery slope, and clinging to her poles, wobblingly started down to them. She did not get very far.

"Keep practicing, Flossie," Nora called out, encouragingly. "You're doing fine."

Toby went over to where a group of boys were bent over the old gasoline engine, and by the time he had his skis on, they had coaxed it into noisy life. Toby put on his mittens, and reaching up, grabbed the moving rope, while the others stood for a moment to watch him being pulled slowly upwards. Mrs. Snow and a wistful Dinghy watched too, from inside the car. They had all decided

that the deep snow would be much too tiring for Dinghy's short legs, and Toby was sure he might even freeze his paws.

"Not bad at all," commented Mark, after Toby had reached the top of the slope. "I see the clan is gathering." He nodded toward the lake which they could just see through the bare trees. "Let's push on."

"I do wish you'd let me leave you off at the academy," Mrs. Snow said. "You'll be soaked."

"Don't worry about us. The snow's not that deep." Mark waved back to her, as he started to break a new trail beside the ski run.

"But at least I could leave your knapsacks and jugs at the school. The jugs are so heavy," Mrs. Snow persisted.

"If there were no hardships it wouldn't be a polar expedition." Nora laughed. "Good-bye, fare you well, Mrs. Snow. Bye, Dink."

As Nora and Star followed Mark and Ted up the slope the hard way, the girls were singing.

"Our anchor's aweigh and our sails they are set,
Good-bye, fare you well; good-bye, fare you well!
And the ones we are leaving we leave with regret.
Hurrah, my boys, we're outward bound!"

Pen and Charley were standing alongside a big snowman, watching a group of boys and girls belly-whopping on their sleds down to the lake and across it. They waved to the expedition when they caught sight of it.

"I'm going all the way to the top of the hill and see the sunset before I put on my skates," Nora said, as she stopped alongside them, and dropped her knapsack and skates on a bench improvised of wooden boxes with a plank thrown across them.

"Let's all go," suggested Pen.

So two more members joined the expedition.

"Just look at those colors!" Nora breathed, after they had reached the summit and were facing the western sky which was painting the glistening snow pink.

And as they all silently watched, the blue of the cove became bluer, and the pale pink of the sky deepened to rose, though the sun was bursting into flame around the edges. Then in minutes the rose paled to lavender, and the flame died down.

Toby, who had loaned his skis to Harvey, came over from the ski run with Ralph Bergman, just as the sun pulled all the color and what little warmth it had been giving out of the sky and over the rim of the Sound.

"Gee, that makes me wish I were a little kid again. Look down there." Toby pointed to where two of the teachers, using tea trays for sleds, were giving the very small children rides down a little slope to the lake. When the trays hit the ice, sometimes they would spin around and tumble the little children off. But that only seemed to add to the fun.

"That gives me an idea!" Ralph started off in the direction of the academy. "When I get back I'm going to put some of you guys to work."

"They're building a bonfire at the edge of the lake near where you left our stuff." Toby shivered in the sudden cold. "Let's get down to it. I'm going to have me some hot chocolarity before I do any more skiing."

And while they were slipping and sliding downhill, the bonfire was touched off, and the flames leaped and glowed skyward as though trying to make up for the sun's desertion. The heat felt good as the skaters sat on the bench, lacing up their skates with chilly fingers.

Mark was the first to glide away, and as Pen watched him swooping, turning and leaping, she shook her head. "He must have been born with skates on."

Nora laughed as she started off. "He looks like a sea gull sailing down wind. Come on, the ice is perfect."

Mr. and Mrs. Sizer, who had come to watch the fun, had brought an old victrola with them. So some of the boys and girls, who either had no skates or were resting, took turns winding it up and changing the records. And very soon the crowd on the ice paired off and were gliding, cross-handed, in time to the music, over the dark ice under the bright-faced moon that hung above the Community church like a lantern placed there for the express purpose of lighting up the party.

"Hey, Ted!"

Nora and Ted, who were waltzing together, looked over to the bank. Ralph was back, standing beside the fire with a rocking chair to which ropes had been attached. And as they skated toward him, Mrs. Sizer tucked two of the little children into it under a warm robe.

"I get it!" Ted laughed as Mark and Charley glided up to them. "Who wants to play horsie?"

And in a moment, to the little children's vast delight, they were flying across the ice behind a span of swift steeds.

Since all the small children had to have rides in the "sleigh," it was fortunate that there were so many relief horses on the ice that evening.

As soon as Toby saw charcoal glowing in the two outdoor fireplaces, he realized that he was very cold again and very hungry. "Avast, messmates!" he yelled to Flossie and Spike. "I'm starved. Stack the skis in the snow, Harve. I'll go ahead and cook us a couple of puppies."

Soon the skaters, attracted by the smell of roasting frankfurters, were crowding around the fireplaces or toasting their hot dogs at the end of long pointed sticks. And when Nora, after looking around, decided that the academy rations looked rather slim, it dawned on her why Mrs. Snow might have packed so much food for them, so the knapsacks and jugs were passed around.

However, after Mrs. Sizer, who had impressed on her large family the fact that they were the hosts that evening, saw their appetites beginning to flag, she came up with a little treat. And in a few minutes, the guests were standing around while poppers were being shaken over the embers in the fireplaces. Then someone started a Christmas carol, and the popcorn seemed to pop in rhythm as they sang. One carol led to another, and as Mrs. Sizer and two of the teachers led the sleepy little ones off to bed, they had the warm look all hosts have when they are giving a successful party.

Toby and Harvey were standing, facing the lake, and tossing the buttery white bubbles into their mouths, when Toby happened to glance below. "That looks like a fire down there!" He pointed to a little flickering light down near the cove. "Hey, Mark!"

Mark left the group around the bonfire and joined them. "What gives?"

Toby pointed again. "Is that a fire down there or someone with a flashlight?"

"You couldn't see a flashlight this far away. It's probably a traffic blinker."

"There isn't one down there," Harvey said. "That's Coveside Road where Star lives. Only I think that's nearer the Weils' house—but I'm not sure. Anyway, it seems to be gone now. They were probably just burning trash."

Toby crammed the rest of his popcorn into his mouth and wiped his hands on his ski pants. "I tell you what," he said when he could talk again. "I'm going to ski down there. I've been wanting to try the golf course. I can go right down to it—if it is the Thurstons' place. Mrs. Snow can pick me up when she leaves Star off."

"Okay." Mark nodded. "But don't try to ski across the road or you'll come a cropper—if not a corpse—and watch out for thin spots."

Toby lunged off with Harvey after him. Harvey had become an ardent ski enthusiast during the last few days and he did not want to miss the sight of Toby flying down the slope.

"Where's Toby, Mark?" Nora and Star were taking off their skates when Mark got back. "We ought to be getting over to the academy. I told Mrs. Snow we'd be waiting for her there."

"Toby's skiing home—at least down to the cove."

Nora turned and looked. "Is that a fire down there?"

"I didn't think so at first, but it sure looks like one now. Hey, Ted!" Mark saw that Ted had his skates off. "Fire down there! Better cut along to the academy and put in an alarm."

CHAPTER 9

Toby let out a war whoop as he started over the smooth blanket of snow that covered the golf course, just for the sheer joy of leaving his ski tracks on its crisp whiteness. Then he burst into a rather unmusical rendition of *White Christmas* as he swooped in a wide Christie to the right and back again to the left across the glinting path the moon was making. He wanted the slope to last as long as possible. He broke off his song long enough to murmur, "Thank you, ma'am," as his skis left the snow and he sailed over a hump. When he had come back to earth, he glanced down to see how near he was to the road and drew in his breath, sharply. The little flicker of light they had seen from the lake, and which he had completely forgotten, was now flaring up in orange flames. Without any more detours, he shot straight to the bottom of the slope, and unfastening his skis, jabbed them in the snow and scrambled up the bank to the road on all fours.

When he got to his feet, Toby started at a run, his boots clattering on the frosted pavement. From this distance, it looked to him as though it might be the Fleets' house that was on fire. Then an awful thought occurred to him—what if it were the carriage house! He was shouting "HELP—FIRE," at the top of his lungs, as he pounded past the Thurstons', though their windows were dark and silent, for now he could see plainly that it *was* the carriage house that was on fire. The flames, shooting up from the far end of it, were making the fitful shadows of the bare-branched trees dance on the snow all around him, as he raced along the driveway. He noticed that the Fleets' windows were dark too, but though he tried to yell "Fire" again, all that came out was a croak. If only a car would come along! His breath was whistling in his chest as he stopped short and watched the flames licking greedily at the old shingles. What if it were *Scud* that was in there. . . . He had to put in an alarm!

He was pounding on the Fleets' back door when he heard the spine-chilling wail of the fire siren calling the volunteer firemen to the firehouse. Someone else must have seen the fire, but it might take ages for the firemen to get there. Toby had once seen a barn burn up practically in seconds. He shuddered now as he remembered the frightful squeals of a horse that had been trapped inside. He pounded the door harder and kicked at it with his boots. Nothing but silence greeted him. Maybe they were all asleep. He turned the door knob and pushed, but the door was locked. "So nobody in Kewanaka ever locks their doors," he was muttering bitterly to himself when he felt heat on the back of his neck. He whirled around. Flames were now reaching over to lick at the roof of the garage attached to the house. Dashing down the steps, he futilely kicked and threw snow where the fire seemed thickest. If he only knew where to find a hose. . . . He yelled again, hoarsely, then stopped to listen, and though the only sounds he could hear were the angry crackling of the flames and the moaning of wind through the trees, he had the eerie feeling that he was being watched. He stood quite still and strained his eyes and ears. The night was so silent, yet full of sound; so dark and yet so bright. He looked up at the sky where thin mist was gathering, blotting out the moon and the stars. The wind was hauling around to the east, blowing the fire away from the carriage house toward the Fleets' and lighting up the back windows. He had to rouse them or they might all be burned up in their beds. As he stumbled around to the front of the house he still had the feeling that eyes were following him and when he looked back and saw a dark shadow that was there one moment and gone the next, he felt a prickling sensation all over. He tried to yell again, but his throat was so dry no sound at all came out.

"Clang—clang—clang—"

The persistent warning of the fire engine came faintly to his ears as Toby mounted the front steps. He relaxed a little. The volunteers had got to the firehouse fast! Nevertheless, he pushed the doorbell with his thumb and kept it there, and banged on the door with his other fist.

"CLANG—CLANG—CLANG—"

Toby took his thumb off the bell and stopped banging. It had just occurred to him that only the fireplace end of the carriage house seemed to be on fire. Maybe the firemen could help him haul the *Mary Christmas* out in time. . . .

Acrid smoke was making his eyes smart and his throat ache, as he plowed his way around the big building and pulled the doors open. He went inside and turned on the lights. The *Mary Christmas* was sitting in her chocks as smug and self-satisfied as when they had left her that

afternoon. Letting out a sigh of relief, Toby went over and put a hand on her cabin top, then lifted his head. The clanging had suddenly stopped, and men's voices had taken its place. The firemen were here!

He was just about to go out for help when Ted's father came in hauling a heavy hose with which he began to spray the fireplace wall. He looked oddly different in his fireman's helmet and shiny black slicker and boots.

"How did you manage to get here so soon?" he asked Toby. "I thought all of you were still at the lake."

"I skied down over the golf course." Toby was tugging at the *Mary Christmas*. "Could some of the men give me a hand? I think we should haul the boat out of here."

"She ought to be able to float herself out soon—like the ark." Mr. Chase smiled wryly. "I hate to flood you out like this, but you can't take chances with a fire."

"She'll be all right where she is, Toby." Mr. Thurston was there, rubbing a sooty wrist across his eyes. "But if the wind hadn't shifted, it might have been a different story. You can shut the water off, Ed," he went on to Mr. Chase. "Looks as though there's no major damage done here—that is nothing that some new shingles won't cover. The garage got the worst of it."

"Who put in the alarm?" Toby leaned wearily against the little boat.

"Mr. Sizer."

Toby nodded. "I thought so. We saw the fire start from the lake. Gosh, it was like a desert around here when I arrived. I banged on the Fleets' door and yelled—I even tried to get in—but I guess no one's home. I wonder how the fire got started." He was mopping at his face with the inside of his watch cap, for though the night was damply cold, perspiration was dripping off his nose.

"Mr. Fleet was in his office on the other side of the house, and he's quite deaf," Mr. Chase was telling him, when a tall, thin, rather stooped old man came in stamping his galoshes.

In his black hat and old-fashioned looking overcoat with the collar turned up, he looked like one of the dark, storm-twisted giant gnomes in Mr. O'Brien's back yard. But not a friendly gnome. His eyes were glittering angrily, and his mouth was a thin hard line under his gray mustache.

Although Toby had never seen Joel's grandfather, he guessed immediately who he was.

"Ha!" the old man exploded, his eyes darting around, fiercely. "They tell me the fire's out, but it started here. Who started it is what I want to know." His eyes darted to Toby. "These children who have turned this place into a shipyard? I told my daughter-in-law they'd be sure to set it afire before they were through. I just gave you permission to store your boat here, Thurston. I didn't—"

"We did *not* set the carriage house on fire!" Toby's face was scarlet with indignation as well as from the massage he had been giving it. "We're very careful about the stove. The fire must have started outside. You should be able to see that for yourself—er-sir." Toby gulped and pointed. "And it couldn't have been sparks from the chimney because we've never even had a fire in the fireplace."

"What's the boy mumbling?" Mr. Fleet put his hand up to his ear. But just then another of the volunteers came in holding out a partially charred stick of kindling toward him.

"Unless you were burning rubbish, Mr. Fleet," the man shouted, "it looks like the work of a firebug. Smell this."

"Burning rubbish at this hour?" Mr. Fleet snorted as he took the stick from him. However, his head snapped back as he sniffed it. "Kerosene! But that's tommyrot! Why should anyone want to set the carriage house afire? Ha!"

"Maybe just to watch it burn," the man shouted, then lowering his voice said to Mr. Chase, "or it could be a spite fire—you know—someone the old man's chiseled on a deal or something—"

"Someone the old man's chiseled, eh?" Mr. Fleet's thick gray mustache fairly bristled. "I'll have you know—"

But what Mr. Fleet would have him know, nobody learned that night, because the fireman had stumbled out of the carriage house almost on the run, muttering to Mr. Chase and Mr. Thurston, who were hauling out the hose, "I always thought the old man was deaf."

Toby was looking toward the pile of kindling that he and Spike had piled beside the stove that afternoon. Now there were only a few sticks lying on the floor. He clapped a hand to his forehead as a sudden thought occurred to him—Joel hated his grandfather, and he didn't like them either! Maybe by setting fire to the carriage house, he had figured on killing two birds with one— "I bet I know who did it," he shouted after Mr. Fleet. "I just bet it was—" He stopped short as Mrs. Fleet came in wringing her hands, and Mrs. Snow was with her.

"Oh, oh," Mrs. Fleet moaned, going up to Joel's grandfather. "This is dreadful—how—when—"

"If you'd been at home where I thought you were,"

Mr. Fleet interrupted, testily, "you might have seen the fire in time to have prevented it spreading—not that I'd have cared if this old place went up in smoke. Ha! It's no good for anything any more, but now I'll have to have a new garage built and most of the back porch."

"But—but—I told you at supper I was going to the lake to fetch Joel."

"Then why isn't he here?" Mr. Fleet asked, sourly.

"I—I don't know. That is he—he—didn't go skating, I guess. Though I fixed him a nice supper to take." Mrs. Fleet's hands were fluttering like moths.

Mr. Fleet snorted again as he stumped out, his hands clasped behind his back.

"Never mind, Ida May," Mrs. Snow comforted. "The place is covered by insurance. You'd better make yourself a hot cuppa and get into bed. On second thoughts, I'll go with you and make tea for us both." She put her arm around Mrs. Fleet's shoulders. "This water should be mopped up before it freezes," she said to Mark and Nora who were standing outside with Star and Ted.

"We'll take care of it." Mark nodded. "It's not too bad, but the wood will have to be dried out before we can work with it. Let's pile it around the stove."

"I'll get a mop," said Star, "and bring back some cider and doughnuts. I'm parched."

"I'll go along to carry the tray." Ted followed her out.

"Something's very rotten in the state of Denmark," Toby confided to Mark and Nora. "That fire was deliberately set. One of the firemen said so. And I know who set it."

"Oh, for pete's sake! You're not going to play that record again!" Mark dropped an armful of wood on the floor. "Isn't it about time you changed it?"

"I don't know what you mean—"

"Oh, yes, you do!" said Nora. "You were just going to tell Mr. Fleet that Joel set the fire when his mother came in, and I'm surprised you had the grace to stop then."

"Well, he did do it. He even had the nerve to use Mr. Thurston's kindling."

"Then why didn't he rescue his outboard?" Mark nodded toward it, racked up on the wall.

"Because—because—well, gee whiz! That would have looked too suspicious."

"Nuts! Where's your proof?"

"Proof! How much more do you want? When I got to the fire, I had a feeling someone else was around, but he didn't show even when I was yelling for help. Once I even thought I saw him, but—"

"Thought! You don't think." Mark sounded disgusted. "All you do is jump to conclusions."

"Well, he wasn't at the lake, was he?" Toby stuck out his chin. "And he was supposed to be. You must have heard what his mother said, and—"

"He could have gone to the movies and eaten his supper there. Come off it, Tobe. That's a serious accusation and you might get yourself into trouble." Mark laughed as he added, "But remind me to tuck a fore 'n' aft cap and a magnifying glass in your little sock, Christmas Eve, *Sherlock*."

"I'll get proof if it's the last thing I do—and it won't just be circumstantial, either." Toby strode out the door, his nose in the air, and almost bumped into Star and her mop.

"Aren't you staying for eats?" she asked him as he started away.

"No, thank you. I have more important things to do."

"Oh, dear!" Nora bit her lip. "We've really hurt his feelings."

Mark shook his head. "Toby couldn't stay sore long if he tried."

"I know," agreed Nora. "That's why I'm so surprised at this—this—*thing* he's worked up over Joel."

Star shrugged. "Joel affects lots of people that way. He'd make a saint want to choke him. Some of the teachers have all they can do to keep their hands off him, and he's a good student, too."

Toby was feeling discouraged as he shuffled through the snow to see the damage the fire had done. Then he heard a little yelp. Dinghy, up to his neck in a drift, was trying to get to him. When Toby leaned over to pick him up, by the light streaming from one of the windows, he saw a small blob of color on the snow. It was a white match cover, decorated with a bright red lobster. He started to drop it in his pocket for Flossie, when a tiny bell of memory sounded somewhere inside him. That was the match folder he had started to pick up when Joel . . . He turned to go back to the others, then stopped. "We'll keep this to ourselves, boy," he whispered to Dinghy as he went on around the carriage house.

Spike was back there standing near the pile of debris the firemen had ripped off the buildings. "This sure was one flop of a fire," he said, when he caught sight of Toby. "Didn't even last till we got here. Did you get here in time to see any of it?"

Toby nodded. "I was here even before the siren went off." Then he added, carelessly, "But you could see even then nothing much was going to happen." He dropped his voice. "You know what, Spike? Joel set that fire."

"Joel! What for?"

"Well, I have a theory, and I know I can prove it." Toby explained about what the fireman had told them, and, after looking carefully around, dropped his voice again, mysteriously. "Is there a restaurant around here called The Lobster?"

"Yes, it's down on Main Street. It just opened a few weeks ago. Why?" Spike sounded puzzled. "Has it anything to do with the fire?"

"It sure has. They'll probably be closed by now, but I'll meet you after school, tomorrow, and we can go there then." Toby straightened his shoulders. "I'll show them! I'll have more than circumstantial evidence against him before I'm through investigating. Come on, I've got to pick up my skis. I left them down near the Weils'. See this?" He put Dinghy down under a street light. "This is the match folder I was picking up in the train when Joel stepped on my hand, *and I found it near where the fire was started.*"

"No kiddin'! But maybe lots of people have them by now."

"I already thought of that, but not many people in Kewanaka eat in restaurants—only summer people. We may draw a blank, but it's worth investigating."

Then for a while nothing was said as they tramped on. Each was apparently busy with his own thoughts.

"Oh, gosh!" Spike finally exclaimed. "It's raining. There

goes the skiing if it keeps up. Did you pay Al and Ralph for your share of the gasoline they burned up?"

"Yop. I had to pay Flossie's share too, but I'm going to make her pay it back. Did Mrs. Snow bring you down from the lake?"

"No, I thumbed a ride with Mrs. Fleet. She thought Joel had been at the wing-ding." Spike grinned in the darkness. "When I told her it might be her house that was on fire, boy, did she step on it. It was like riding in a hot rod."

"Have you ever ridden in a souped-up rod?" Toby asked him.

"No," Spike admitted, reluctantly.

"Here we are." Toby stopped. "Keep Dink up there." He slid down the bank. "Catch hold of my skis and help me up," he said a moment later, and after he had been hauled to the top of the bank, puffing, said, "Star's handing out cider and doughnuts. Maybe there'll be some left when we get back."

"The parents were at the Weils' playing bridge when the siren went off, so they were at the fire when I got there. They took my skis and told me to meet them there," Spike explained, regretfully. "But maybe they'll be having eats. We'll drop you off at the Fo'c's'le if you want."

"No, I think I'll go back." Toby scooped up a handful of clean snow and put it in his mouth. "I'd like some of that cider. My throat feels like a nutmeg grater."

"Okay, goof." Spike started to amble along.

"Now remember, Spike, not a word of this to anybody. Understand? Not even to Flossie, she blabs everything she knows."

"I'll say she does! See you tomorrow outside of school."

124

Spike sounded interested in playing Watson to Toby's Sherlock.

As he turned away, with Dinghy trotting close to his heels, Toby was wondering how he could go back to the carriage house and still save face. I'll tell them— Gosh, all I have to tell them is I had to get my skis!

CHAPTER 10

ALTHOUGH IT HAD RAINED and stopped and rained again the night of the fire, they woke up to a frosty fairy world the next morning. Nora caught her breath when she looked out her window. Under the deep blue sky, each frosted twig of the maple trees shone like silver wire, and the red berries on the prickly bushes alongside the house twinkled like tiny Christmas tree lights. She could hardly wait to get outside before the sun had a chance to change it all.

At breakfast, Mrs. Snow, seeing Nora's eyes return again and again to the windows, proclaimed a holiday. "This is no morning for young people to stay indoors, drying dishes or doing lessons," was what she said. "You've been working so hard on this and that ever since you got here, it's time all of you had a day off. So scat!"

Nora looked at her gratefully and hurried to put on her boots and coat. She already had on her winter jeans. She would go down the bluff to the beach. But as she ran down the back steps, she had to stand on the lowest one and touch one of the little Christmas lights and the ice seemed to burn her finger tip. Then she broke through the crusted snow along what was a path in summer. Everything around was silver-sheeted, and when little gusts touched the branches of the trees and shrubs, everywhere there was the sound of tiny silver bells. The fir trees were as splendid as Christmas trees with their silver ornaments.

The path ended in a narrow strip of sandy beach that was golden in summer, but now was plated with silver too. She stood with her face to the wind, drinking in the smell of salt, and listening to the screech of gulls, circling over her head. The earth was white, and the gulls were gray on top, but white underneath, and the sea was blue, edged with the white lace the wind was whipping up as far as the eye could reach. And the blue sky with its white scud trimming matched the sea. Nora smiled to herself as she remembered that upstairs in her closet hung the dress that she was going to wear to the yacht club dance, and it, too, matched the day—blue frosted with silver.

After a time she began to feel chilly, and stamped her feet to warm them while she tried to decide where to go next. She would go to the cove. Then she had to choose whether to climb back up the bluff or go around the point on the beach. She decided to stay on the beach.

The wind had whipped her cheeks to crimson by the time she had reached Mr. O'Brien's cheerful cottage. She knew he would not be home, but she went down the steps and around to the back to see what his birds were doing. Even the dark, twisted giant gnomes were splendid in silver livery this morning, and the sun was beginning to spangle their branches with little shiny beads of silver too. She held her breath when a curious jay lighted on a branch over her head, and after satisfying himself that she was not an enemy, he cocked his head and began to preen his blue jacket, as though calling her attention to it.

She looked down at the creek when he had flown away.

Their friends the black ducks—she was sure they were the same—who, last summer, used to swim out to *Scud* to be fed, were now floating in a shallow pool out of the wind. She wished she had thought to bring along some bread for them, but she had not known that she would be finding them there in winter. Then she had an idea, and reaching into her pocket for her pencil and the little notebook she nearly always carried with her, so she could jot down ideas for the poems and stories she might write, she let herself into Mr. O'Brien's neat kitchen. Tearing out a clean page, she wrote, "I am helping myself to some of your bread for the ducks," then signed it and anchored it down with the salt shaker.

She found the breadbox and took several slices, since there was almost a whole loaf left.

The ducks looked at her with interest as she climbed down the bank, and crowded, greedily, as they watched her pull the bread apart.

"You remember me. I'm sure you do," she told them as she threw bits first to this one and then to that, because, if you were not careful how you fed them, some were bound to be left out. After she had tossed the last crumb, she held up her hands to show them they were empty, and most of the ducks turned their backs ungratefully. But three of them lifted their wings and soared low over the pool in a straight line, giving her a view of their lovely shadows reflected in the water, as though to reward her for her bounty.

She was thinking, as she climbed the seven steps back to the road, that she was glad she had finished making her Christmas presents before they had left the city. Now all she had to do was wrap them. She had knitted a lavender stole for Mrs. Snow, and argyle socks for Father and the boys, and had written jingles to go with them. She would go around to the dime store and buy wrappings and ribbon for the boys too. She felt in her pocket to be sure she had her purse. It was there.

When she reached Coveside Road and saw little Benjie Weil trying to make a snowman all by himself back of the house, she remembered that he had been ill, and had not been around to learn his song. So she walked back there to help him roll the big snowball for the body.

"Hi, Benjie, boy," she said. "I'm glad you're well again."

But the little boy whirled to face her, his eyes making two panic stricken O's in his rosy face. "I didn't mean it," he whispered. "It—it just spilt." Then he pressed the palms of his mittened hands tightly over each eye, but if he was crying, no sound escaped him.

"He thinks if you can't see the tears, you won't know he's crying." Benjie's mother whispered. She had seen Nora from the window and had thrown a coat over her shoulders and come out.

"Is he well again?" Nora was whispering too.

Mrs. Weil shook her head. "Dr. Adams says there's nothing wrong with him—physically, that is. He says he's sure that he has something on his mind. He also told us that unless we can find out what it is, he might be really ill."

Nora frowned in perplexity, then suddenly her face cleared. She squatted down alongside the little boy, but did not touch him. "You mean that horrid old green paint?" she asked him.

"It—it just spilt itself." Benjie's shoulders were heaving.

"I know." Nora's face was solemn. "Paint has a nasty

129

way of doing that, like—like milk—and when you least
expect it to."

"But Toby—" Benjie choked. "Now he won't want me
to help him."

"Oh, yes he will. After all Toby's—" Nora stopped. She
had been about to say, "practically a little boy himself,"
but decided that sounded somehow disloyal, so she sub-
stituted, "Toby's always spilling paint too—all painters do
sometimes. Don't you remember his green hair?"

Benjie moved a mitten so that half of one big brown
eye showed and regarded her unwinkingly, then the
mitten covered it again. "But Joel told me not to touch it."

Nora had to lean very close to hear.

"He—he opened the can for me and told me he'd bring
me a toy boat he got when he was almost six and—and I
could paint it. He—he said he was going to bring me a

little brush he had too." Benjie's shoulders began to heave again as he wailed, "But I wanted to paint a real boat with a man's brush."

"And that's just what Toby wants you to do tomorrow." Nora straightened up, and Mrs. Weil put a hand lightly on her shoulder. "We're not working today because the firemen had to hose the inside of the carriage house, and it's still damp in there."

"Daddy's one of the firemen and he said the *Mary Christmas* isn't burnt at all." Both of Benjie's mittens came down from his eyes.

Mrs. Weil bent over and wiped the round, tear-streaked face with her apron, murmuring, "Benjie Weil, you have snow all over your fat cheeks, and Jack Frost will nip them if we don't dry you off."

"Let's make the snowman fat too." Nora waved to Mrs. Weil who went back into the house, wiping a suspicion of moisture off her own cheeks.

"We've decided to paint the hull white again, the way it was," Nora said, cautiously, as she and Benjie made a path across the yard with the snowball he had made. "That's more like Christmas, you see—white for the snow and green for the Christmas tree." She had remembered the smear of green on the boat.

"What will be red for holly berries?" Benjie stopped pushing to think.

"I know," said Nora, hastily. "We'll tell Star that she and Port should always wear red sweaters and red caps when they go sailing."

"You have good ideas." Benjie went back to pushing again. "I like *some* girl sitters."

✦

131

Santa Clara County Free Library
San Jose, Calif.

Mark went out the front door that morning with a package under his arm. As he stood in the road looking out across the bay to the Sound, he too, was feeling the magic of the trees that had turned to silver overnight, and the wind that made the branches tinkle and was whipping the Sound into a froth. It was one of those magic mornings in any season when a man with a boat longs to set sail with only the horizon for his goal.

Winter cruising! he thought to himself. That would be something. On and on, far off the coast, maybe even to Newfoundland—to Port aux Basques. He savored the foreign name as if he could almost taste it, and was seeing that bleak northern haven crowded with sturdy fishing boats, and peopling them with hardy, hard-bitten, foreign-looking fishermen in woolen caps. His would be a sturdy vessel too—a schooner with a beautifully curved clipper bow and husky bowsprit, with a tall raked mainmast made of Oregon pine—and tough sails too, that could weather the northwest gales. He shivered, almost feeling the driving snow and sleet biting through his thick clothing. But soon his hour's trick at the wheel would be over. Then down below to the steaming cabin to gorge himself on thick, meaty stew and boiling hot tea, while one of the hands played sea chanties on an accordion.

As he passed the shipyard, he came back to reality, and a fleeting sense of depression stole over him, for he was remembering that no more would yachts be in the making there. He pressed the package under his arm and grinned a little to himself as he pushed on. Inside the package was a vessel of his own making—and it was a schooner too. It was Toby's Christmas present. Last summer Mr. Gardiner had taught him the trick of getting a sailing vessel into a bottle, but he wanted him to be on hand to supervise the launching.

Though Mark enjoyed feeling the *Mary Christmas* change under his hands and according to his plans, he really liked making miniatures best—like the model of *Scud* and the bottle boat for Toby. He had carved some little gulls for Nora, each one perched on its own small piece of driftwood, so that she could arrange and rearrange them as she liked. And he had carved three much larger ones, flat on the back, so that Mrs. Snow could fly them across the paneled wall over the fireplace, above the pewter mugs and tankards that were the color of the sea when fog closed in.

He opened the gate in the picket fence that ran in front of a low white building, the back of which, he knew, was one big window that looked out on nothing but sky and water. He peered through the glass-paned door. Mr. Gardiner was bent over his drawing board.

Toby had spent his morning wandering aimlessly about and thinking dark thoughts. He had never tried to be a detective by himself before—well, practically by himself— Spike didn't really count. He was much more interested in skiing. Toby had thought of going to The Lobster by himself, but had vetoed the idea when he remembered that he had promised Spike he could go with him. Maybe he'd better get back to the house and finish Mark's Christmas present. Mark himself had taught Toby how to temper steel into a fine blade, and the shop teacher had helped him design a sturdy little knife with a smooth wooden handle that just fitted the palm of the hand—the perfect knife for a model builder. But there was the handle to stain and varnish. So he cut short his walk and hid himself in his room with strict orders to Mrs. Snow to warn him of Mark's approach.

"I shall stand by the window like Sister Anne, Sister Anne," she had assured him.

Mark was still not there when Nora came in, so she went upstairs to tell Toby about Benjie and the mystery of the green paint. "We should have guessed something like that," she said, after she had knocked on the door and identified herself. "Remember Joel had something under his arm wrapped in newspaper when he came in that day?"

Toby, who was sitting cross-legged on the floor, nodded, bleakly. There goes my second best clue up the chimney, he was thinking.

"The knife is beautiful." Nora guessed from his expression something of what was going on in his head. "Do you want me to hide it under my bed till it dries?"

"Please."

"What's that over there?" Something bright lying on Toby's bed had caught her eye.

"Don't look!" Toby scrambled to his feet and sat down on it.

"I'm sorry, Toby. I know you should never pry at this time of year. I didn't really see it." He's made me one of those tiles his class has been firing in the school kiln. Nora smiled to herself as she went out.

But Nora was wrong. Toby had not made the tile for her. He had made it for Flossie, just in case she had a present for him—which he felt sure she would have. However, if he had guessed wrong, he had planned to give it to Nora for her birthday. He pulled it from under him and looked at it, admiringly. On the highly glazed blue background, a ship that was supposed to be *Scud,* was sailing over bright green, very uniform waves. He had bought a fine small pinseal notebook for Nora, and had fastened to the cover one bronze and two silver musical notes, which anyone with any imagination at all should know meant any kind of notes.

If Nora had told Mrs. Snow and Mark about Benjie, it must have been privately. At any rate, the subject was not brought up during dinner, and when Toby met Spike after school, he did not mention it either.

The Lobster was open when they walked in, but there were no customers there. A sleepy looking man, sitting at the desk, rolling a toothpick around in his mouth, looked at them as they stood stamping the snow off their boots on the mat.

"We don't start servin' again until five-thirty," he told them.

"We didn't come to eat today," Toby said. "We—we just want to ask you something. Did this match folder come from this place?"

"Yeah." The man took it from him and opened it. "Or maybe it didn't. This here's like the samples they gave us."

"Samples?"

"Yeah. Match salesmen carry them with them when they're tryin' t' sell ye a bill of goods. See?" The man picked up what looked like a duplicate from a box on the desk, and opening it, showed that there was printing inside, whereas Toby's was blank. "An' see this?" The man turned the folder over. "We got our address printed on the back. What's it all about, kid?"

"Well," Toby began cautiously, trying to remember what he had planned to say. "You see, I collect book matches, and if you could autograph this and put a date on it for me, it would make it very valuable to my collection. You know, like—like first editions of books," he ended lamely. He was not very good at telling untruths.

"Yeah? Sure, I'll oblige." The man took a fountain pen from his inside pocket. "An' you can do me a favor by tellin' your folks an' everyone what an elite place we're runnin'. I'll even give ye a menu an' autograph that too. Do you collect them?"

"No, we don't," said Spike, "but it's an idea. I'd like one."

Toby frowned at him. He wanted to keep the man's mind on the matches. "How many of these samples did you give away?" he asked him.

"I don't think we give none away. We only had a couple. That's why I'm wonderin' where you got hold of this."

"I found it," Toby said, quite truthfully, "and I'd sort of like to know how many more people have them."

"Hey, Uncle!" The man raised his voice. "Come in here a minute, will ye?" He turned back to Toby. "He's m' uncle," he explained, when a man in a chef's hat pushed open a swinging door at the back and poked his head through. The man at the desk talked to him, haltingly in a foreign language, and "Uncle" stood scratching his chin for a moment, then answered him rapidly in what sounded like the same language. "He don't catch on t' English is why I gotta talk t' him in Greek," the man confided.

"It sounded like Greek to me." Spike giggled.

136

Toby jabbed him with his elbow. "What did he say?"

"He says he don't remember givin' none away."

"Oh." Toby's face fell. "Well, thank you, anyway."

"What date d' ye want me t' put down?" The man was carefully writing his name on the inside of the folder.

"Oh—er—er—the date you opened the place, I guess."

Toby had lost interest in the transaction and stood lost in thought, while the man dated and autographed the menu for Spike.

"Don't forget you're gonna advertise this place for us," the man said as they made their way to the door. "Business ain't so hot. Maybe we shoulda waited t' open when the tourists start comin' through. Hey! Wait up a minute—"

Toby paused with his hand on the door knob. The chef's hat was again poking through the door, and after saying something, "Uncle" quickly withdrew it.

"He says he remembers now givin' a coupla samples to a guy from old Fleet's who comes round t' collect the rent—when we're mor'n a day late," he added, bitterly.

"We know him. Thanks Mr.—Mr.—" Toby opened the match folder—"Mr. Pappas. We'll advertise this place like everything for you," he added as he opened the door. "Do you realize," he said, excitedly, to Spike when they were outside, "that we've got Joel on ice now? Even Mark will have to see that."

"What are you going to do about him? Go to the police?"

"Oh, gosh, I don't know." Toby had not gone that far in his thinking. He had just wanted to prove his theory to the others. "Maybe it isn't proof—I mean definite proof that we could pin on him. I mean, for instance, you and I collect the things for Flossie, and maybe Joel collects them for someone else."

"Joel!" Spike exploded. "That guy wouldn't give you the time of day!"

"Anyway, maybe we'd better hunt for more evidence." Toby hunched his shoulders. "Something strong enough to—to wring a confession out of him."

CHAPTER 11

CHRISTMAS APPROACHED nearer and nearer. The day
Sam came home for the holidays and strolled into the
carriage house made everybody realize that there was
no time to be lost if the *Mary Christmas* was to be
ready to make her debut as a cruising sloop Christmas
Eve, and if the program was to be a success. Then the
schools in town let out, and the carriage house became a
beehive of industry from morning till night.

Now it was only two days before Christmas Eve, and
the last piece of trim was in place, the last drop of paint
and varnish hard and dry. The brightwork gleamed, the
tools were all back where they had come from, and the
carriage house was swept clean. But such is habit, many
of the shipbuilders found themselves dropping in there,
especially late in the afternoon.

So when Mrs. Snow pulled open the doors that afternoon, although the big room was already sliding into
silver, it looked very cheerful in there. Spike and Harvey
were roasting apples at the end of pointed sticks over
the glowing coals in the old pot-bellied stove on which a
pan of chestnuts were roasting too. Toby, with Flossie
and Dinghy looking on, was brushing luminous paint on
the blade of the wicked-looking knife that Mark would
brandish in the play, and Toby's nose was twitching like

a rabbit's as he sniffed the lovely aroma of hot chestnuts. The older ones were just talking.

"Is Sam here?" Mrs. Snow asked.

"No, he isn't." Ted got up and offered her his seat on the porch swing. "He's taken Pen off on a mope in the family car."

"No, sit down, Ted. I can't stay. I just wanted him to try on his bishop's miter before the dress rehearsal tonight." Mrs. Snow held it up.

"Why not try it on me?" Ted sat down again. "We wear the same size hat."

When Mrs. Snow, standing in back of the swing, placed the miter on Ted's dark head, Nora burst out laughing.

"If Sam had ears like the Mad Hatter's," she said, "it might stay up."

"It just needs a little tuck here in the back," Mrs. Snow said through a mouthful of pins. "Here, put on the beard while I fix it, so I can get the whole effect."

Then when she had anchored the tuck with her pins, Ted again modeled it for her, and she nodded. "It'll do. Ted, I want you and Mark to come along with me to load Mrs. Fisher's melodeon into the car. And the rest of you had better get started soon for the rehearsal."

"Are they having the rehearsal on the bandstand?" Flossie asked.

"Of course not, lame-brain." Toby was tossing a hot chestnut from hand to hand to cool it. "Then anyone who wanted to could come and see it tonight instead of Christmas Eve when they have to bring gifts. We're having it in church."

"I never thought of that." Flossie showed most of her

shiny gold wires. She never seemed to mind what Toby said to her as long as he said something.

"So you'd better toddle along home, since you're not in it," Spike told her.

"Oh, stop it, Spike!" Star leaned over and flicked the back of his head. "She can come to the rehearsal if she wants to."

"Let's go." Ted, still wearing the beard and miter, pushed open the doors and then lunged forward. He had all but knocked down old Mr. Fleet and had reached out to steady him.

Mr. Fleet angrily brushed off the hands that were clutching him. "Can't you look where you're going? Ha! Can't even feel safe on my own property since you—" He broke off short as Ted stepped back. "What kind of fool masquerade is going on here?"

"There's a dress rehearsal for the Christmas program tonight," Mrs. Snow put in soothingly. "Give me the hat and whiskers, Ted."

"Ha! You're the one I came here looking for." Now Mr. Fleet was glaring at Mrs. Snow. "Thought I saw your old rattle-trap pull in here. What's the meaning of this?" He waved a sheet of paper in front of her face. "Where's Ida May gone to? What is she up to now? Why isn't she in the kitchen getting my supper? Ha! Well, read it, woman, read it!" He snapped on the lights.

Mrs. Snow calmly took the paper from him while the others looked on in silent amusement. They knew that it would take more than old Mr. Fleet to floor her.

But there was a look of bewilderment on Mrs. Snow's face as she read the typewritten note aloud: "Joel and I have gone away for a while. I am sure you can have your meals at the Fo'c's'le until I get back. Ida May."

"I'll bet Joel found out we were investigating him," Spike whispered to Toby, "and is running away."

Toby nodded. He was sure of it. He placed a warning finger across his lips.

"Doesn't even say how long she's going to be away or where she's gone. Ha!" Mr. Fleet's head was thrust forward, as his eyes raked Mrs. Snow's face. "But you know. She tells you everything."

"Not quite everything, it seems, because I don't know. And there's no use speculating. You'll know as soon as Ida May chooses to tell you, I expect. I have three other guests staying with me"—she indicated Mark, Nora and Toby—"and their father is coming for Christmas, but you're welcome to have your meals with us if you like. Supper's not till seven-thirty tonight because of the rehearsal, and dinner's always at one."

Mr. Fleet was looking at the Brices, sourly. Suddenly he jabbed a finger in Toby's direction. "He looks as if he hadn't been brought up to know that mealtime's for eating and not for gabbling. Ha! I'll take my meals at the inn."

"Good!" Toby muttered to Spike.

"Very well, then." Mrs. Snow pulled her driving gloves from her pocket. "But remember, the inn doesn't serve very good meals out of season."

"I'll at least have them in peace and quiet the way I'm used to." Mr. Fleet turned on his heel.

"Poor Joel!" murmured Nora. "No wonder he's peculiar."

"There's that new restaurant on Main Street called

The Lobster," Toby shouted after him, suddenly remembering his promise to Mr. Pappas. "It's very elite."

Mr. Fleet turned around. "You don't have to shout, boy. I'm not deaf. Ha!"

"Then it's very funny, sir, that you didn't hear me when I rang and pounded and kicked on your door the night of the fire."

"The fire! Ha! Yes, the fire. Do you know what it cost me to have the garage and the carriage house—"

"We really have to be going, Mr. Fleet." Mrs. Snow motioned to Mark to close the door after them. "If you change your mind about having your meals with us, just come along. There's always enough."

"Are you taking Dinghy to the rehearsal with you?" Flossie asked Toby after Mark and Ted had left with Mrs. Snow.

"Uh-huh. The custodian's nuts about him. I promised him I'd bring him."

More snow had fallen, and there was still plenty of it on the ground to light up the earth. The icy frost on the pavement crackled under their feet as they tramped down the road on the way to the church, and Christmas was in the air all around them. Since they were early, they took a detour along Main Street across which, high overhead, lights were blowing in the wind, and the shops glittered like bright colored candy fruit. The scent of the Christmas trees stacked up in front of the florist shop was as heady as Christmas wassail. Toby and Flossie ran on ahead to look in the gift shop window where old, asthmatic Mrs. Collins was winding up monkeys in scarlet caps. When she put them down, they would bob back and forth, clapping their cymbals together.

That is where Mark found them after they had left Mrs. Fisher and the melodeon at the church. "Did you remember to bring my knife?" he asked Toby.

"Holy grommet! I forgot all about it. Is Mrs. Snow and her jalopy still at the church?"

Mark shook his head. "She went home to start supper. I'll run back and get it."

"No, I'm the one who forgot it—I'll go back. They can rehearse the pageant first if I'm late." Toby started down the street at a gallop, and Dinghy had a hard time keeping up with him.

He was nearing the Fleets' place, when a car came down the road behind him. As it passed under a street light he caught a glimpse of old Mr. Fleet bent over the wheel. He lagged back when he saw it pull up alongside the walk that led to the office at the side of the house. Toby was wishing he had not mentioned the fire to the irascible old man, and was not going to give him a chance to bring it up again if he could help it. When he saw the tall, stooped figure disappear into the shadow of the walk, he stepped along more briskly and glanced down at the office just in time to see the door open and a light flash on. Why he stopped for a moment to watch Mr. Fleet, he could never explain afterwards even to himself. But he did stop, and while he watched, a red-and-black plaid arm flashed in the air, and as quickly flashed down. He heard an awful groaning scream as the light went out and a door banged shut inside.

Toby stood rooted, with Dinghy cowering at his feet, growling softly. Joel hadn't gone away! He had just killed his grandfather! Maybe he had written that note himself. He remembered that it had been typewritten. Then he heard feet clattering down the front steps, and as if of their own volition, his legs were carrying him along the walk toward the office. Joel was running away now, though! He had to try to do something for the old man if he wasn't dead yet. "You stay outside, Dink," he whispered. His hand was shaking as he pushed the door farther open. He had never seen a dead person. "Mr. Fleet," he said in a low voice. "Are—are you alive, sir?"

A dull groan answered him.

He wasn't dead yet! But Toby was frightened anyway as he looked around to adjust his eyes to the darker darkness of indoors. He did not want to turn on a light, but in a moment there was enough light reflected from the star-lit snow to show him Mr. Fleet, lying on his face on the floor beside a big desk on which there was a telephone. Carefully stepping around the long, dark figure, he picked up the hand-set and tried to remember Spike's number, but could not. So, pushing his finger into the last hole, he spun the dial.

"Operator," a bored voice said.

"This—this is an emergency." Toby's teeth chattered as he tried to talk just loud enough for her to hear him. "Old Mr. Fleet on Coveside Road has nearly been killed in his office. Tell Dr. Adams he'd better get here fast. Jo-Jo—"
For some reason, the name Joel stuck in his throat.

"What are you saying? Speak a little louder, please." The operator sounded impatient.

"Tell Dr. Adams to be quick. Do you understand?"

"Yes. Who's speaking, please."

145

"Toby Brice, but that doesn't matter. I'll stay until the doctor gets here."

After he had hung up, Toby looked around again. Across the room was a closed door which evidently led into the house—and which was probably the door that he had heard slam—and beside it was a big safe, its door gaping open. Mr. Fleet must have surprised Joel in the act of robbing his safe. Then he remembered what Ted had told him about Mr. Fleet and banks. If this was where he kept all his money, there must have been plenty in it. . . .

Mr. Fleet groaned again, and Toby knelt beside him for a moment. The man's black hat was still on his head, but it was crushed in. Toby shuddered. He wanted to ease him into a more comfortable position, but knew it would be better to leave him as he was until Dr. Adams came. He stood up again and suddenly felt as though he were going to be sick. He opened the door and drew in a great lungful of crisp, cold air just in time. He closed the door behind him and stood breathing deeply and listening for a car. Nothing around him but silence—the same way it had been the night of the fire. He felt even more alone now than he had then. He would phone Mrs. Snow! She'd know what to do until Dr. Adams came. He put his hand on the door knob again, but did not turn it. He would get Mr. Thurston. Why hadn't he thought of that right away! Feeling better now that he would not have to go back in there alone, he ran around the office to the back—the shortest way to the Thurstons'—but as he was passing the carriage house, he noticed that the doors were open. He knew that they had left them shut. Maybe Joel was hiding in there. . . . He stood, hesitatingly, when Dinghy came flying out and landed on his back in the snow, yelping. Toby saw red. Joel had kicked his dog! Without stopping to think, he picked Dinghy up, and charging inside, snapped on the lights. "You big bully!" he shouted at the figure in the red-and-black plaid mackinaw that was bent over the outboard racked up on the wall.

The figure whirled, and the lights were snapped off, but not before Toby had recognized the Mad Hatter with his brown felt hat resting on his big ears. Then the man's fist caught him on the side of the head and sent him reeling.

"It's you again, you interfering little whelp!" the man snarled.

Dinghy, barking shrilly, tried to wriggle out of Toby's arms.

"And keep your mutt quiet, if you know what's good for both of you."

"Hush, Dink. It's all right," Toby whispered, and though Dinghy stopped barking, he was trembling violently.

Toby's thoughts were reeling too. It was the Mad Hatter Mr. Fleet had surprised robbing his safe. Gosh, you'd never think to look at him he'd have the nerve to attack anyone. If Mark had come back for the knife instead, he wouldn't have dared to clout him. . . . Toby's mouth tightened as he started to walk toward the door, then he stopped and drew in his breath. Did the man know he'd seen him knock out old Mr. Fleet? He must try to act casually. . . . He strolled over to the table where the wicked-looking knife glowed in the dark. It looked anything but wicked to him now as he picked it up. "I came back from the rehearsal at the church to

147

get this," he said, hoarsely. "I—I guess I'd better be getting on."

"Put that thing down," the Mad Hatter bleated.

Gosh, he sounds almost as scared as I feel, Toby was thinking, and his voice was almost normal as he said, "It's only wood."

"I don't care what it is. Put it down, anyway, and stay right where you are or—or I'll really let you have it."

Maybe if he could do something to attract Mr. Thurston's attention. . . . Toby leaned over and looked out the window, but the Thurston house was dark. He'd just have to—

"Can you run this here outboard?" The Mad Hatter's whine cut in on his thoughts.

"S-sure." Again Toby was finding it difficult to act offhand. "We have one on our boat and I'm in charge of it."

"You can take me across the cove in Joel's dink then. I—I got a date over there and I'm late. That way you can bring it back too, so no one'll think I tried to steal it." The man snickered softly.

"I couldn't do that—Joel wouldn't like it."

"Joel ain't going to know about it. He and his old lady have gone away for Christmas, he told me."

"But the rehearsal," Toby said, weakly. "I have to get back there or—" He stopped because the Mad Hatter had moved out of the shadow and was now standing in the doorway, balancing a murderous looking length of iron pipe, menacingly.

Toby's heart turned a somersault as he thought of the crushed black felt hat on Mr. Fleet's head. That was probably the weapon the man had used. He swallowed hard. "I—I have to see how badly you hurt my dog first,"

149

he quavered, setting Dinghy on the table and running his hands over him. He had to try to leave a message in case Mark came to see what was holding him up. He looked around the table, but the only thing on it, besides the wooden knife, was one of the unused paint rags.

"The mutt ain't going with us. You're leaving him in here."

In the dim light, sifting through the windows, Toby saw the man pick up a can, and as he leaned over the outboard, the reek of gasoline was strong. Now while the man's attention was diverted, maybe he could get away. Holding tightly to Dinghy, he started to tiptoe toward the door.

"No, you don't!"

As the can was set on the floor with a clatter, Toby's heart threatened another raid on his throat. He put Dinghy down again, and after a frantic search through his pockets came up with a stub of pencil, but he had no paper. Then his fingers closed over the match folder with the red lobster on it.

"Come on, get going. You're leading the way." The Mad Hatter was lifting the outboard from its rack.

"I have to bandage my dog first," Toby said, desperately. "I think you've broken a couple of his ribs."

"Shhh!" The Mad Hatter stepped over to the doorway, listening.

Then Toby heard a car speeding down the road. Dr. Adams, he thought, as it pulled up outside with a screech of tires. If he could only make a break for it now! But he knew immediately that he would not have a chance. The man was blocking the doorway, and he had the heavy piece of pipe in his hand again. Maybe Dink might

150

be able to get away. . . . The nape of Toby's neck crawled as he turned his back on the Mad Hatter, wondering what to write. Then something clicked in his mind. Now he was remembering how the man had greeted him. "It's you *again*—" was what he had said, and then, "You're always underfoot—" It was the Mad Hatter who had set the carriage house on fire and was watching him that night! He hastily scrawled a message on the folder, more by feel than by sight, and clipped it over Dinghy's collar. Then grabbing up the paint rag, he tied it firmly around the trembling little dog. Dinghy was his only hope now. Maybe the white rag would keep him from being run over in the dark.

"Come on, kid," the Mad Hatter whispered. He had the outboard over his shoulder, and was waving the pipe in his other hand.

As Toby started slowly toward him, he was praying for a miracle, and at the same time was whispering, "Home, Dink! Please don't get run over, fella. Find someone. Home!"

The Mad Hatter was standing outside now, still listening, but watching Toby too, and as Toby, with a quick motion, tossed Dinghy onto the driveway, the man's foot shot out to kick the little dog back inside. But Dinghy eluded him and shot around the corner of the building, whimpering.

"You did that on purpose!" The Mad Hatter snarled.

Out of the corner of his eye, Toby saw him raise the pipe, and ducked to one side to avoid it, then started to run. But the man's foot shot out again, and tripped him up.

CHAPTER 12

SAM AND PEN were driving to the church when Pen let out an exclamation.

"Careful, Sam! Don't hit that skunk."

Sam slowed down as a pair of eyes at the side of the road glittered in the headlights, and he saw the small black and white animal. Then he, too, let out an exclamation and braked the car to a stop. "Skunks don't usually go in for horizontal stripes," he said. "That's Dink and he seems to be in costume. Has he a part in the program too? One of the black sheep, no doubt."

"Really, Sam, your humor gets worse and worse."

Sam laughed as he stepped out on to the road shouting, "Hi, Toby!" He picked up the little dog, who yelped when he pressed him close. Sam shouted again and looked up and down the road, but there was no answering shout. "That's odd," he said, climbing back into the car. "Wherever Dink is, Toby's always on his heels or vice versa." He handed him to Pen.

"There's something wrong!" she exclaimed. "He's trembling all over."

"Let me take a look at him." Sam leaned over, and in the light from the dashboard, pressed the little body, gently, while Dinghy whimpered. "This seems to be a crude attempt at a bandage. Snap on the overhead light."

He unknotted the bandage, and picking up the little dog, went over him carefully. "No bones broken," he said, finally. "My guess is that he's been kicked, and I think he's been badly frightened."

"Just being kicked would be enough to frighten him." Pen took Dinghy from him. "I don't believe he's ever been kicked in his life. You don't suppose anything's happened to Toby, do you?"

"I don't know." Sam was frowning. "I wish we knew where Dink was coming from. He seems to have been heading for home."

"Maybe we'd better turn around and take him back to the Fo'c's'le," said Pen. "Look, here's something on his collar. It's a match folder." She detached it.

"George Pappas." She was reading inside. "Who's he?" She shrugged, then turned the folder over. "There are dim pencil marks on the back." She held the folder closer to her eyes. "I can just make it out. 'Spike not J— Mad H. Sand bar S O S, S O S, S O S.' Toby and his codes!" Pen laughed. "Remember how keen he was about them last summer? Nora told me he was sure Joel had deliberately set the carriage house on fire, and has been trying to prove it. Spike is probably sleuthing with him, and this is Toby's dramatic way of sending him a message."

Sam shook his head. "It doesn't quite add up. Toby would never send Dink off by himself—especially in the dark. I don't like this. Let me see that folder." Sam took it from Pen and read it himself. "Except for the S O S's, this is no code. Not J— that could mean Joel. Mad H.— I don't get that."

"The Mad Hatter—that's what Nora calls Ferd Snively," Pen explained.

153

"Sand bar—" Sam shook his head again. "Well, let's get to the church. If it doesn't mean anything, both Toby and Spike should be there by now."

When they got there, Spike, looking very bulky in the blue hooded jerkin he was wearing over his ski suit, was standing in the vestibule of the church with Flossie. They were watching for Toby.

"Where's Tobe?" Spike asked when he saw Sam was carrying Dinghy. "He's holding up the works."

"What kind of games have you boys been up to?" Pen handed him the folder. "Here, read this under the light. It seems to be for you."

"Not J— Mad H. S O S—" Spike read in a puzzled voice. "Gee, I don't know—" he turned the folder over. "Yes, I do! Toby found this on the scene of the crime—I mean at the fire, and we thought it was Joel's. Well, anyway, he must have found out some way that the Mad Hatter set the carriage house on fire, but I don't get this sand bar routine. Toby forgot Mark's knife and went back to the carriage house to get it."

"See?" Pen looked at Sam. "I told you they had been sleuthing."

"That doesn't tell us where Toby is or how Dink got hurt."

"Dink hurt?" Mark, in his costume, had come out to look for Toby.

"Not badly. I think someone must have kicked him, but he's more frightened than hurt." Then Sam explained about finding Dinghy and the message attached to his collar.

Mark took the folder from Spike, and as he read it, his brows drew together. "Sand bar! It can't mean he's *on* the sand bar, and if he found out, some way, that someone is hung up there, why didn't he telephone for help? He must be in bad trouble to have sent Dink off alone—"

"What is it, Mark?" Now Nora with Star and Ted were there, and others were crowding around.

"I think something's happened to Toby. Is your father home, Star?"

"No, he's in the city—working at the university."

"We have to get down to the cove and get hold of a boat some way." Mark was pounding his palm with his other fist.

"Why?" Nora's face was white under her stage make-up.

"Get into the car. It's across the road. Here!" Sam thrust Dinghy into Mark's arms, and turned to the minister, who had come out to see why most of his cast had disappeared. "Mr. Winslow, would you please call the harbor patrol? And phone Conor O'Brien too. Tell him to have the *Monica* at the shipyard wharf and ready to go. Go with him, Pen, and explain—but hurry. Then commandeer a car and take some men to the carriage house. Search the beach— Oh, and check on Joel's dinghy," he shouted after her, then sprinted down the steps and across the road.

Sam gave a quick glance around when he got in the car. In the front seat were Mark, Nora and Dinghy, and in the back were Star, leaning forward so as not to crush her angel wings, the Ethiopian king, King Melchior, with Flossie on his lap, and two of the three little boys crouched at their feet.

"What was that about Joel's dinghy?" Nora asked him as he started the car.

"Well, Mark's right, of course. When Toby sent that

155

message with Dink, he must have been on land, and if he went out to the sand bar afterwards to rescue someone, he might have taken Joel's dink—because that's the only boat on the beach down there." Sam was driving fast, but carefully.

"But if he was in such an all-fired hurry to get out there, why bother explaining about Joel and the Mad Hatter?" Mark was leaning forward, tensely. "And you could tell by his writing he was in a hurry. It looked as if he'd written it in the dark."

Sam glanced at him. "Don't worry. Wherever Toby is we'll find him fast. If Conor isn't home when Mr. Winslow calls, I'll take one of our workboats. I have my keys to the yard. How long has he been gone?"

"At least half an hour." Nora's voice shook.

"Don't worry, Norie." Mark tried to relax in order to reassure her. "Tobe can always take care of himself."

"But out on the cove at night in that little boat, alone, and it's so cold—"

Sam drove a little faster.

As Toby started down the path to the beach with the Mad Hatter at his heels, his heart was in his throat again. If it had been a dark night, he might have made another try to get away and lose himself among the trees. But between the lopsided moon, the bright stars and the snow, the night was almost as light as day. He could hardly drag one boot after the other as they came to the beach, and he stopped in front of the dinghy shed.

"Keep going!" The Mad Hatter prodded him between the shoulders. "I already tied the dink up at the end of the wharf." He sounded nervous. His shifty little eyes

156

were darting here and there and he seemed to be listening.

But whatever he was afraid of, Toby thought, drearily, it wasn't of him. The Mad Hatter was armed now with two weapons—the iron pipe and the outboard, either of which could be used to dash his brains out. How did the man figure he was going to get away with this? But he must have figured out something because he'd planned his get-away ahead of time. . . .

Now they were going down the wharf, and Toby concentrated on willing the Mad Hatter to step into a hole and, at least, break a leg. But the short journey was uneventful, and all too soon they were picking their way down the rotting steps that led into the water.

The Mad Hatter put the motor down, and standing with it between his feet, pulled in the dinghy which had been tied up to the steps, and made Toby get into it first. Then thrusting the iron pipe into the pocket of his mackinaw on the side away from Toby, he slid into the boat himself and reached for the motor. "I've put this here outboard on the dink plenty of times for Joel," he confided, and he did not sound nervous now. "I could even run the thing, I bet, but seeing as you're an expert—" He gave a bleating little snigger, then went forward to cast them off the wharf and haul in the line. He did not toss the starting cord at Toby's feet until he had sat down across from him and forward. "Get her going and no tricks!" The man patted his pocket, suggestively.

Toby had left his mittens on the table in the carriage house, and now he slowly drew his cold hands from his pockets and turned up the collar of his pea jacket. For the first time in his life, he was not happy in a boat. He was breathing quickly, as though he had been running. He was sure that once they were across the cove, the Mad Hatter would not let him live. After they landed, he would probably knock him out too, and maybe even sink the boat with him in it to make it look like an accident. . . . He gritted his teeth, hoping the motor would balk, and that somebody might hear them and come down to see why anyone should be out on the cove at night in the dead of winter, but it turned over at the second try. If Dinghy were found, would anyone understand his message? His original idea had been to drop the centerboard and run up on the sand bar if he could, but he realized now that that would be suicide—he might get a soaking and freeze to death before they were found. Maybe the harbor patrol . . .

"What do you think you're doing?" The Mad Hatter's shrill bleat broke into Toby's thoughts. "I want you to take me to Captain's Landing, and that's over there."

Toby, who had been heading out toward the Sound, swerved the boat sharply, and the man threw himself to the floor boards with a terrified yelp.

Toby swerved the boat again, shipping a bucketful of water aboard.

"Don't do that!" The Mad Hatter screamed over the sound of the motor. "I—I can't swim!" He was on his knees, clutching the seat with both hands.

"You and me both, brother, on a night like this!" Toby muttered, grimly, but leaned over and started to unlace his boots, just the same. Oh, gosh! If Mark were here, he'd know what to do! With sudden courage, he shouted, "Toss me that hunk of pipe and toss it gently or I'll tip you right in."

158

For a moment the man did not move. Then his hat blew off, and his head jerked around. Without his hat, he looked somehow indecent and more menacing than ever. And when, still on his knees, and clinging to the seat, he began to make his way slowly aft, Toby's little burst of courage oozed away.

"Look, Mr. Snively," he yelled. "Can I help it if the wind and tide are acting crazy? If you'll just go back and sit 'way up in the bow, it will help balance the boat." He held his breath. Would the man really believe that?

The Mad Hatter stopped for a moment, his little eyes watching him. Then raising himself cautiously to the seat, and without taking his eyes off Toby, he began, as cautiously, to slide himself forward.

Toby knew that for the moment he had won; that the man believed him. Relief so intense flooded over him that for a moment he could not speak. Then he nodded as if the little victory were of no importance. "Okay," he said, "I'll have to head out toward the Sound again though and slowly circle back, so as to keep us on an even keel." But though the man just sat there, clinging to the gunwale with both hands, wordlessly staring ahead, any hope left him that Dinghy would find his way home, and that Mrs. Snow would understand the message and send a boat to find him in time. Once they landed . . . He shuddered, wondering how long the gas would hold out. Throttling down the motor, he put a freezing hand to his ear and listened. He thought he could make out a faint hum in the distance, but that might just be a plane. Then his mind seemed to freeze too, until he looked down, dully, at the water swirling over his boots. He'd better finish unlacing them. Maybe he'd have a tiny chance if he capsized the boat near shore. Then he could kick off his boots—kick off his boots—kick off his boots—

"Start in now and keep going slow!"

Toby's head jerked up at the Mad Hatter's shout. "Sure," he was trying to say, when he noticed that the humming sound he had heard earlier had become louder, and looking out toward the Sound, he saw two lights—one red and one green—coming in around Eastern Point. With sudden hope, he shouted at the top of his lungs though he knew that he probably could not be heard over the noise of their engine.

"Who is it?" the Mad Hatter screamed, as Toby slowed down almost to a stop.

"The harbor patrol, I hope." Toby's voice was shrill.

"No, no!" The Mad Hatter jumped up, then gave a terrified bleat, as the little boat heeled, shipping enough water to almost swamp her, and sank to the floor boards just as the other boat beamed a searchlight on them.

Mrs. Snow was right, Toby thought, as he waved the boat toward them, now he knows he's 'ad it, he's all bleat and no chin!

"Ahoy!" the man, running the powerboat, sang out from the wheelhouse. "Are you the Brice kid that's missing?"

"Yes!" Toby shouted back, cutting off his motor as the other boat slowed down alongside them. Then scrambling forward, he tossed the towline to another man, who was putting a fender over the side. "You're the harbor patrol, aren't you?" he asked him.

"That's right. What's this all about?" The man was pulling the dinghy closer. "We got a call that someone had run aground on the sand bar."

Toby, who was now clinging to the rope on the fender, grinned stiffly. Good old Dink! He had made it. Then he sobered. "I'm sorry to get you out on a cold night like this, but this character clobbered old Mr. Fleet over the head tonight. His name's Snively. Mr. Fleet caught him robbing his safe."

"I only took what I figgered he owed me," the Mad Hatter whined. "He—he fired me, and I couldn't get another job."

"And he stole Joel Fleet's mackinaw," Toby went on, "so that if anyone saw him hanging around, they'd think Joel did it."

"I did not!" The man's voice was loud now with indignation. "Joel's old lady gave it to me herself, when I told her I had to hock my overcoat."

"Why did you set their carriage house on fire a couple of weeks ago?" demanded Toby, but the Mad Hatter relapsed into sullen silence. "He probably was trying to lure Mr. Fleet out of his office so he could rob him then. He used to work for him so he probably knew the combination." Toby was looking up at the patrol. "But I spoiled his little game for him that night too— Hey, here comes another boat!" Over the throbbing of the powerboat's exhaust, he had heard the steady chug-chug-chug of a boat putting into the cove.

The man in the wheelhouse came on deck and turned the searchlight on it. "It's Conor O'Brien's *Monica*," he said.

As it came closer, the Mad Hatter got to his feet, and Toby had all he could do, clinging to the fender of the patroller, to keep the little dinghy steady.

"Who are they?" the man was pointing, and his teeth were rattling like castanets.

It was a strangely assorted crew leaning over the rail of the *Monica* with anxious faces. Between the two tall kings in their jeweled crowns, a pair of angel's wings fluttered in the wind.

Toby looked at the Mad Hatter over his shoulder. "That's the Prince of Darkness come to take you across the Styx," he told him, nodding toward the Ethiopian king. "The angel probably came for me."

The men in the patrol boat laughed as they hauled the shivering Mad Hatter aboard.

"You'd better take him below and roll him in a blanket if you want to save him for the chair," Toby suggested. "He must be plenty wet. And watch out for that hunk of iron he's packing—it's the murder weapon."

"Murder!"

"Well, I don't know if Mr. Fleet died, but his head looked kind of sq-squashed." Toby shuddered, not only at the recollection, but because the cold wind was turning his wet feet to ice. "I put in a phone call to Dr. Adams, but I couldn't stay because the Mad H—this guy kidnapped me."

"You going back with the angel?" one of the men asked him.

"I'll say!" Toby grinned up at him.

"Okay, Skipper. We'll empty the dink and tow it around for you."

The first person Toby saw when he reached the deck of the *Monica*, was Mark, holding Dinghy.

162

"Doctor Livingstone, I presume." Mark was looking at him closely.

But Toby only took Dinghy from him and buried his cold fingers in his warm fur.

"You made us miss the rehearsal." Nora spoke sharply, though her hands were clenched at her sides. She was very near tears, and wanted to put her arms around Toby and comfort him the way she used to when he was much younger. Although she did not know why, she sensed that he had been through a bad time.

"I know." Toby's voice quavered. Reaction had set in, and suddenly he was very tired, and was feeling a little sick again. "I—I couldn't help it. Is Mr. Fleet going to pull through?"

"Mr. Fleet?" The others, who had crowded around, looked at one another.

"Come along in and stop badgerin' the lad with questions." Mr. O'Brien had put his head out of the wheelhouse door. "He's prob'ly cold an' starved." Then when Toby was inside, Mr. O'Brien looked him over and nodded his head. "Ye don't seem t' be damaged none by whatever it is y've been up t'—no topmasts gone, at any rate, though yer sails look like they could do with a flap in the sun."

"Got that tea brewed yet, Sam?" Ted called down the companionway.

"It's all poured and I'm putting a shtick in it," Sam's voice floated up from below.

"Stick?" Toby looked interested as he scrambled down the companionway, carrying Dinghy. He felt he never wanted to put him down again.

"Conor says there's nothin' loike shtrong tay laced with

limon to ward off the pew-monia." Sam came out of the galley and handed him a steaming cup.

"Oh." Toby sat down on one of the berths and took a sip. The hot, thick cup felt good to his numb hands.

"Get your clothes off." Mark was in the cabin now. "I'm going to heat a blanket and wrap you up in it."

Toby pulled off his cap and started to unbutton his pea jacket. "I'm not very wet. My ski pants are waterproof."

"Strip off everything anyway." Mark was on his knees tugging at Toby's boots.

"The Mad Hatter!" Mark shook his head. "I shouldn't have thought he'd have had the nerve. He looks like such a rabbit. But maybe even rabbits bite when they think they're cornered."

Toby, considerably refreshed by several cups of tea and many sea biscuits spread with peanut butter, had explained his part in the evening's adventure, and the others, between bites of hardtack and gulps of tea had explained theirs.

Toby was propped up under the blankets on the port berth, in one of Mr. O'Brien's woolen shirts, with Dinghy snuggled under his arm. And although the little dog was not permitted to lie on berths, even Nora, who was sitting on the foot of it, was not reminding Toby of that. Flossie and the angel were sitting on the starboard berth with two of the little boys. At least Flossie and the angel were, but Spike and Harvey kept hopping up to spread more hardtack and pour more tea. Mark and the two kings preferred to stand, rolling to the motion of the boat, but Sam was sitting halfway up the companionway steps to relay the highlights of Toby's story to Mr. O'Brien.

"Anyway, it's lucky you had a chance to phone Dr. Adams before Snively grabbed you," said Ted, after Toby had run down.

"And don't worry about Mr. Fleet," Spike put in. "My dad will patch him up good as new, I bet."

"Ferd Snively will be deservin' everything he gets," a voice boomed unexpectedly from the wheelhouse. "Fer all he huffs an' puffs an' likes t' have his own way, Mr. Fleet is not an unkindly man. He fired Snively when he discovered him jackin' up the rents an' pocketin' the difference, but he give him another chance workin' at the garage where he immejately started dippin' inta the till. An' even then the old man didn't set the law on him, because Snively's mother is a Fleet. She's prob'ly no relation, but it's mighty proud he is of the Fleet name."

"Gosh, I just happened to think!" Toby exclaimed. "The Mad Hatter said he only took what he figured ought to be coming to him, but if Mr. Fleet keeps all his money in that safe, maybe he got quite a haul—I mean if Mr. Fleet never puts his money in the bank."

"Where did you get that idea?" Sam asked him. "He keeps his money in the Kewanaka bank, the same as everyone else around here does."

"Oh." Toby looked at Ted, but he was innocently polishing his nails on his royal robe.

"I think it's just wonderful the way you solved the mystery of the carriage house fire, Toby." Flossie was looking at him, admiringly.

"By a fluke," growled Mark.

"Don't say that!" Toby shuddered. "Flukes are sort of flounders, aren't they?"

"Correct—of the genus flatfish. Why?"

"Well, gosh, I don't believe I'll ever be able to eat a flounder again. For a time there I thought I'd be at the bottom of the cove with them nibbling on me for a change."

"That's too bad," said Nora, "because that's what we're having for supper tonight—stuffed with shrimp—the way we had them the night we arrived."

166

"Well—" Toby thought for a moment. "I can pick out the shrimps."

"Get on the line, Sam. We're in," Mr. O'Brien called out.

Spike pressed his nose to one of the portholes. "Pen and Mrs. Snow are waiting for us on the wharf. I'll go and ask them if they know anything about Mr. Fleet," he said, as Mr. O'Brien killed the engine. Then in a few minutes he was back, putting his head through the wheel-house door. "He's going to be okay," he said, "but Dad took him to the hospital to have him X-rayed just to be sure.

"The hospital!" Toby whistled. "I'll bet he's hacked."

"Shhh!" That was Nora, who was following the others up the steps. Mr. O'Brien was talking to Mrs. Snow, and she wanted to hear what he was saying.

"—safe an' sound," he was booming, "but just t' be on the sure side, I'm keepin' him aboard t'night—an' the wee Dink too."

"Yippee!" Toby hugged the little dog closer, and Dinghy yelped. "Oh, gosh, I'm sorry, Dink. I forgot about your sore ribs."

CHAPTER 13

CHRISTMAS EVE came in, in the traditional way, with frost and snow on the ground, and a bright blue sky overhead. And the little town of Kewanaka never looked or sounded happier. Main Street was bustling with excited children and their beaming mothers going to the markets to buy the Christmas feast, swinging their shopping bags or trundling their wire carts before them. Almost everyone wore a sprig of holly or mistletoe on their coats, and the shopkeepers were grinning from ear to ear.

No sooner were the breakfast dishes put away in the Fo'c's'le that morning than they heard Ted's whistle out front, and joined him to walk to the village where they were meeting Star. There was a tree to be selected for the carriage house as well as for the Fo'c's'le, and greens and wreaths to be bought.

Several letters had passed between Mrs. Snow and Mrs. Thurston, and as soon as her guests were out of the way, Mrs. Snow became very active in the kitchen preparing the feast the Thurstons were giving that night in the carriage house for all their friends to greet Port.

When Mark and Nora had gone to the *Monica* to see Toby, the morning before, he seemed to have quite recovered from his harrowing adventure, and today, with the whole world sparkling around him, he could only think of Christmas.

And that evening, after the sun had set, the feeling of Christmas seemed more intensified than ever, for the night brought with it a galaxy of brilliant stars. The Milky Way had never seemed so close, and Venus, at her brightest, obligingly hung over the conical roof of the bandstand just as the Star of Wonder must have hung over the stable in Bethlehem so long ago.

Now all around the village green, volunteer traffic directors, with white arm bands, were directing the traffic one way, and soon the green in front of the stage was jammed. Bunchy little children were lifted to the tops of cars in order to see better, but the older ones and their parents were crowded around, stamping their feet in the snow, their breath steaming the air like so many kettles on the boil. And important girl scouts and boy scouts were scattering through the crowd, for they were to announce the arrival of the Christmas players.

Mrs. Snow's station wagon was off to one side of the bandstand, banked with evergreen boughs on the audience side, and little Mrs. Fisher was already inside, seated in front of her melodeon, warming her fingers.

Ted's father had gone to the station to meet Mr. Brice, and they were almost the last to arrive. Latecomers would have to leave their cars at a distance in order to keep the streets around the green as quiet as possible. They had no sooner found a place to stand that commanded a view of the stage than the faint jingle of sleigh bells could be heard in the distance.

"The Christmas Players!" All the scouts' voices rang out

excitedly. "Here comes Saint Nicholas! The players are here!" And others took up the cry, when two stage hands, manipulating spotlights from the branches of two tall trees in front of the bandstand, directed their lights on the other end of the green, where Angelo Guglieri, the man who drove the vegetable wagon, was jingling across the snow-covered pond in an old box sleigh, with the cast of the Saint Nicholas play kneeling in the hay behind him. He was standing with his feet apart, cracking a long whip over the broad back of his fat, white horse, Lucia. He was not whipping her, and she apparently knew he would not, for she kept to the same slow trot—that is until the spotlights were full upon her, when she threw back her head and lifted her hoofs almost daintily. Angelo was in medieval costume too—at least he was dressed very differently than usual. As the sleigh came on, the long tail of his bright green cap whipped in the breeze. He circled the darkened stage once, with the spotlights following him, and the audience applauding wildly. But when he came back, he stopped the sleigh in front of the steps, and the lights faded to nothing. Then the players climbed out, while Angelo unhitched Lucia and led her around back. The sleigh had been left to receive the gifts at the end of the program.

When the lights came on again, Mr. Brice did not at first recognize his son and daughter, who were standing in the hay heaped on the stage in front of three large tubs. Mark had on a rough, villainous looking red wig, and Nora had a dirty scarf tied around her head from which gray hair straggled. Both their faces had been hideously made up.

Everybody laughed—or almost everybody. Some of the

smallest children, sitting on the car tops, were squealing, and their parents had to reassure them.

Then the little melodeon pealed forth, and a hush of anticipation fell over the crowd, before the innkeeper and his wife began to sing with fearful clarity about who they were, and their nasty little habit of chopping up their guests and pickling them in salting tubs to serve up for bacon, and how little children made the best bacon because they were so tender. So when the three little boys came out of the shadows from behind the bandstand and started up the inn steps, the audience broke into low hisses and moans of warning. But the little boys continued to troop up, trustfully, singing, "Oh, please, Mr. Innkeeper, please take us in for the night is so dark and so cold—"

"Come in, little pets. Have you lost your way?" The innkeeper's wife was rubbing her hands together in horrible glee, while her husband leered at the little boys and ran his thumb along the edge of his wicked-looking knife. Then he burst into villainous song, and flashing his knife around his head and into the shadows to make it glow, he chopped at the little boys, who shrieked their fear each time he paused for breath, and as he grabbed them by their scruffs, one at a time, and tumbled them into the tubs. After that he and his wife sang a paean of triumph that consisted mostly of the word bacon, while the good wife sprinkled salt over the little boys, and her husband stirred them up with his knife.

It was while they were at this delightful occupation that old Lucia ambled into the spotlight, and then the audience did break out into roars. Saint Nicholas in his long red robes and tall miter and handsome Turkey red cloak—Mr. O'Brien's travel cloth—was seated sidesaddle fashion on her broad bare back, stroking his long white whiskers and singing, "Ho, innkeeper, innkeeper, where are my boys?" and explaining that he had seen in a vision what had befallen them. He slid off Lucia's back, while the innkeeper and his wife were protesting their innocence, and slapped her sharply on the rump, which was her cue to amble around to where Angelo was waiting to lead her away. But attracted by the hay in the sleigh, Lucia stopped for a snack. And as Saint Nicholas mounted the inn steps, nobody could hear what he was singing because they were roaring again, as they watched Angelo pull the reluctant Lucia away. By the time the audience could hear again, Saint Nicholas was making signs over the tubs, and three blue-hooded heads popped up, one by one, yawning and rubbing their eyes. "Oh, what a lovely dream I had," they caroled together.

"I dreamed of a dear, little pink sugar mouse." The first little boy's teeth gleamed in his dusky face as he waited to hear what the second little boy had dreamed.

"I dreamed of a beautiful gingerbread house," the second little boy sang in a clear soprano.

"I dreamed of a piglet with an apple in its mouth," the third little boy sang, and as usual, he was not quite on key and he did not quite rhyme.

After Saint Nicholas had forgiven the penitent innkeepers, he left them on their knees and stepped to the front of the stage to remind all the little children in the audience to hang up their stockings before they went to bed that night. As he stood, his arms spread out in benediction, the lights slowly dimmed, then went out to show that the play had ended.

172

As soon as the stage was dark, Nora flew around to the back of the bandstand where the cast of the Christmas play were waiting in cars for their turn to go on. She was anxious to get out of her costume and out in front before their play started.

And she was only just in time, for as she wedged herself into the first row of the crowd, the melodeon tinkled to life again, and the angel chorus, grouped alongside the station wagon, out of sight of the audience, started to sing, *Oh, Little Town of Bethlehem,* and everybody joined in, as the lights slowly came on. But when Mrs. Fisher began to play, *It Came upon a Midnight Clear,* an awed hush fell over the audience, and they stood in deep silence, their eyes on the stage where Mary, in her blue robe, knelt behind the manger, the tips of her fingers raised reverently together, and Joseph leaned on his staff, his head bent. Behind a gauze curtain at the back, three angels seemed to be bending down to touch their harps of gold. And over the stable, the guiding star shone bright.

Nora swallowed a lump in her throat. The scene could have been painted by one of the old masters, and made her feel as the shepherds must have felt under these same stars so many hundreds of years ago. Then Mary and Joseph stirred a little, and the three angels sang of the Glory of the Lord, and although Nora had seen or taken part in the story of the Nativity every Christmas since she could remember, it had never so completely absorbed her. It was as though she had never seen it before. When the little children, led by Benjie, came from the inn to the stable where, they had heard, a new little lamb had been born, while they knelt in awe and sang of the Little Lord Jesus asleep in the hay, to Nora they were not chil-

173

Santa Clara County Free Library
San Jose, Calif.

dren she knew, but children who lived long ago. And as the story moved on briefly, but beautifully, with the shepherds and the wise men following the star, the feeling that she was witnessing a beauty out of the past deepened.

The Nativity play ended as it had begun, in a tableau, with the three kings kneeling on the steps offering their gifts, and the shepherds and the little children grouped worshipfully around, while the unseen choir led the audience in *Silent Night*, and the lights dimmed.

When the lights came on again, Benjie was standing in the sleigh, a gift in his hands, and as he sang, *And a Little Child Led Them*, all the scouts crowded forward to place their gifts at his feet. And after Benjie had been lifted down, the audience, singing *Adeste Fideles*, moved up to place their offerings in the sleigh.

When Mark, Nora and Toby, dressed in their best, arrived at the carriage house on foot with Father, the scene that greeted their eyes was truly terrific. Mrs. Fisher was playing her melodeon at a great rate, and everybody else in the place was lined up and dancing the Virginia Reel, with Conor O'Brien bawling the calls. "Both hands around! Now do-si-do!"

The only light in the high-ceilinged room came from candles on the garlanded mantel, and from others set along the long workbench that had been transformed into a groaning banquet board, and the tall Christmas tree glittered with colored lights. There was a fire in the fireplace, and the pot-bellied stove glowed at the other end of the room.

After they had flung their coats on the pile heaped up on the battered table, Nora, her plaid kilt whirling, grabbed Toby and got into the dance. But Mark and Father, their backs to the fireplace, stood for a while warming their coat-tails and just looking on.

"The warehouse was as snug, and warm, and dry, and bright a ballroom, as you would desire to see upon a winter's night," murmured Father.

Mark looked up at him.

His father laughed. "The Fezziwigs Christmas Eve ball. Remember—in *The Christmas Carol?*"

Then Mark remembered and laughed too.

"They're not turning on the lights until Port gets here. And we're all to stay at this end until everyone's been introduced," Toby told Mark all in a rush, as the two lines cast off, and he trotted past them, looking very smart in his freshly pressed gray flannel suit.

"Okay." Mark nodded. He was savoring the delicious combination of holiday scents all about him; of apples and spices and wood-smoke, and the fragrance of smoldering balsam boughs that were beginning to crackle.

Just as Mrs. Snow was gasping that she could not dance another step, there was a loud bang on the door, and the music stopped, while Ted and Sam pushed open the big doors that were decorated with holly wreaths. Then Star, her eyes dancing, came in with Port. And if anyone had asked Mr. Brice to guess which was the healthier twin, he would have been sure to point to Port. Her skin was tanned by the southern sun, whereas the only reminder of summer was a sprinkling of freckles across the bridge of Star's nose. But they had been aptly named. Port was dark and resembled her father, and Star was fair and resembled her mother. Star kept Port's back to the *Mary Christmas,* while their father piled their coats on top of the others.

"There's no use telling Port all your names at once," Star said, "but, anyway, this is Port."

Everyone laughed and called out, "Welcome home! Merry Christmas, Port!"

Then after Mark had introduced Father in almost the same way to the few people in the room he had not already met, the crowd scattered in a semi-circle around the *Mary Christmas,* and the overhead lights were snapped on.

"What happens next?" Father whispered to Nora.

Nora's little dimple flashed as she whispered back, "You'll see."

They had refused Mr. Chase's offer of a lift to the carriage house in order to give Father a chance to brief them on his doings since they had last seen him, and to give them a chance to brief him on theirs. But Nora had decided that they would keep the story of the cabin as a sort of surprise for him too.

Now Star was leading a considerably dazed Port over to the *Mary Christmas,* whose mast had been stepped, and her mainsail furled on the boom and lashed with stops.

Port rubbed her eyes in bewilderment.

"She looks like Sara Crewe," Nora murmured to Father, "the night the Lascar had transformed her room, and she thought the dream had come before she had time to go to sleep."

"And the sloop is Port's dream?" Father nodded toward it. "It's the smallest cruising vessel I've ever seen."

Then Nora explained to him about the transformation of the little sloop.

"So Mark designed the cabin." Father pulled out his tobacco pouch and began to fill his pipe as he moved closer to listen while Star showed it off.

And if Star sometimes gave the impression that from keel to cabin top, the little sloop was of Mark's design and of their building, perhaps it was because Star, like the *Mary Christmas,* had quite forgotten her origin; for the little vessel had changed so gradually and naturally from day to day, it was almost impossible to tell where the old left off and the new began.

"I—I can't believe it!" Port had climbed into the boat, and now she dropped down weakly on one of the lockers.

"Look at the binnacle." Star turned on the offset flashlight that was clipped above a shelf set behind a pane of plate glass. "We'll have to start saving right away for a compass."

Nora saw Mr. and Mrs. Thurston exchange a glance over Star's head, so she felt sure there was a compass in one of the packages piled up under the tree.

"I just don't know what to say—how to thank all of you." Port shook her head as she looked around. "To think I'll be able to go sailing next summer, after all."

"Come below—the port berth's yours, of course." Star stooped and went in. That afternoon she and Nora had put books on the bookshelf, and had hung cups from the hooks in the cupboard, and had piled some plates and bowls under them. Even their little camp stove was sitting on its shelf at the head of Port's berth, so the little cabin already looked lived in.

"You come with me, Toby." Mrs. Snow caught hold

of him just as he was about to follow Port and Star into the boat. "You and Spike are going to be the mullers."

As Toby followed Mrs. Snow to the other end of the room, his eyes feasted on the banquet table which was heaped with so many things he could not see them all at a glance. There were two cold turkeys and a great glazed ham, salads, baskets of crusty bread, cranberry sauce, fruit cakes, a wooden bowl filled with apples, pears and grapes— He scooped up a handful of nuts before joining Mrs. Snow and Spike in front of the wide hearth on which thick mugs were lined up between two big pewter pitchers. "Just what is it, a muller?" he asked them.

"We're having mulled cider," said Mrs. Snow, "and when these pokers that are on the fire are red hot, you plunge them into the pitchers, and that is mulling."

Toby leaned over and sniffed at one of the pitchers, and licked his lips as the delicious aroma of spices floated up to him. He had just mulled his pitcher, when the doors cracked open again, and Dr. and Mrs. Adams came in.

"I'm glad you were able to get here. Doctors are so unpredictable." Mrs. Snow hurried up to the newcomers with two mugs of steaming brew. "You must be cold. Drink this while it's hot. We danced ourselves warm."

"How did the academy make out, Mom?" Charley Adams was taking his mother's coat.

"Way beyond anyone's expectations." Mrs. Adams sipped her cider, appreciatively. She was one of the ladies from the churches who had charge of the gifts. "Mr. Sizer finally got everything loaded into a truck, and the academy is agog with excitement."

"What's going on here?" Dr. Adams' eyes twinkled as he watched Conor O'Brien and Mr. Brice sliding the hatch cover on the little cabin back and forth like small boys with a new toy.

"This is as fine a hatch cover as ever I've seen," said Mr. O'Brien. "A real professional job."

Then as Dr. Adams stooped to look into the cabin, Father turned to Mark who had been watching him. "You'll get that scholarship when you're in M.I.T., Skipper, or I miss my guess," he said and laid his hand on Mark's shoulder for a brief moment.

Toby, who had come up with cider for them, overheard him. "Just wait till you see the model of *Sc—*" He stopped and looked at them aghast.

But if Father and Mark had heard him, they said nothing. Mark, his face flushed, had buried his nose in his mug.

"She's a real little cruiser." Dr. Adams straightened up and pulled the varnished hatch cover over.

"Did you tell them about Joel?" Mrs. Adams asked him.

"Not yet. But it's really your story."

"Joel?" exclaimed Toby. "What about him?"

And others crowded around Mrs. Adams to hear too.

"I'll try to make it brief." Mrs. Adams smiled. "The evening of the skating party at the lake, a friend of ours —an eye surgeon from the city—was visiting us, and when I saw Joel, alone as usual, trudging up the hill with his skates, just on impulse, I persuaded him to come in and have Dr. Whitney examine him." Mrs. Adams paused, reflectively, then gave another quick, little smile. "I said I'd make this brief. This morning in New York, Joel had his first operation—and it was a complete success," she ended.

"I knew that's what they were up to, the minute I read

180

that note Ida May left," Mrs. Snow said. "She knew Mr. Fleet would come running to me with it so that's why she couldn't tell me anything. But how in the world—"

"Persuading Ida May to take the boy to the hospital was probably the hardest job I ever tackled," Mrs. Adams broke in. "But I'm sure that by now she is as happy as he is."

"I declare that's wonderful news." There was a suspicion of a tear glistening in Mrs. Snow's usually merry eye. "He's been such an unhappy boy."

"Gosh, maybe he can get into Annapolis after all," said Toby.

"But what about his grandfather?" Pen asked.

"That's the doctor's story." Mrs. Adams looked up at him, standing alongside her.

Dr. Adams chuckled. "At this very minute, Mr. Fleet is toying with the idea of giving us a new wing for the hospital. When I left him, he was telling everyone he could buttonhole that there's no place like a hospital when you're ailing." The doctor chuckled again as he added, "I think he'll want to have his X-ray pictures framed."

"But does he know about the lad?" Conor O'Brien asked him.

Dr. Adams nodded. "I told him, and he's already convinced that it was all his own doing. I'm driving him to the city tomorrow to have Christmas dinner in the hospital there with Joel and Mrs. Fleet."

"I wonder which of the Three Christmas Ghosts changed him," said Nora.

"No doubt Ferd Snively knocked a bit of sense into his stubborn, old head." Mrs. Snow sniffed. "Come along, folks, I'm as hungry as Toby usually is. Pick up your plates and help yourselves. You carve this turkey, Mr. Thurston. You take on that one over there, Mr. Brice. We'll let you operate on the ham, Doctor." Mrs. Snow was bustling and beaming and handing out plates and knives and forks, as she herded the party into three lines behind the carvers.

When the last mince pie and the last crumb of fruit cake had been consumed, and the table cleared of all but the nuts and candies and the few apples left in the wooden bowl, Mrs. Fisher went back to her melodeon, and the older guests sat on the porch swing and the chairs around the pot-bellied stove, and the younger ones sat on the floor around the hearth, but they all sang the carols that Mrs. Fisher never seemed too tired to play.

At last Dr. Adams looked at his watch and reminded them all that Port had had a long tiring day, and also that there were other trees to trim, and presents to be put out for the morning.

Then Mrs. Adams whispered something to him, and he nodded. "I almost forgot. Joel gave me a message for Mark and Nora. He says you can sail *Fleetsark* in the Christmas regatta, if you like."

"Tell him when you see him tomorrow that we sure do thank him, sir." Mark got to his feet, grinning. "And tell him we'll do our best to keep her out in front for him."

"Gosh, the surprises are coming thick and fast," said Toby.

"You know what?" Spike said, when they went to get their coats. "I bet anything Joel will swap you one of his father's charts now."

"Do you really think so?" Toby grabbed a handful of candy as he passed the table.

"Sure. He may even give it to you. He sounds like a reformed character."

"I have a present for you, Toby." Flossie was standing beside him, her hands behind her back. Then she held out a package. "Merry Christmas."

Toby took it from her and groaned to himself. From the shape of the package, he knew it was a tie—probably a hideous one. "Thank you." Now he would have to give her the tile. Then another thought struck him, and feeling around in the pockets of his gabardine coat, he pulled out the match folder with the bright red lobster on it. "Merry Christmas," he said. "It will be the prize of your collection, because it was really the clue that broke the case, and it saved my life too."

"You're giving it to me?" squealed Flossie. "Oh, thank you, Toby."

"Think nothing of it." Toby thrust the package into his pocket. "I'll bet it's a swell tie."

"Oh, you guessed!" Flossie's face fell.

"Sherlock never guesses." Mark was hunching himself into his topcoat. "Sherlock deduces."

Santa Clara County
LIBRARY

Renewals:

(800) 471-0991
www.santaclaracountylib.org